THE REALITY OF US

VANESSA NORTH

vanessa north
lovers gonna love

PRAISE FOR VANESSA NORTH

"[A]uthentic characters charting complicated paths with grace and courage."

"A beautiful look at female relationships."

"A steamy book in which nuanced friendships are as central as the romance between two star-crossed lovers."

"Steamy and compelling"

"Smooth and sexy"

"[A] fabulous romance with two male leads."

CONTENT ADVISORY

Please be aware that this title contains content some readers may find difficult to read. This includes discussion of off-page in the past gun violence, on-page anxiety attacks, on-page injury, and off-page in the past parental death.

ONE

Alden looked at the subject line of the new message in his inbox and took one long, slow blink before removing his glasses and pinching the bridge of his nose. Maybe, if he closed his eyes and counted to ten, the problem would go away. Like how unplugging his router and going for a Starbucks seemed to fix ninety-nine percent of his computer issues. He opened his eyes.

The message was still there.

Packing lists and partner assignments for team-building weekend

No. Just. No. Okay, so maybe he was in denial. Maybe he had really hoped that by ignoring this, it would go away. He knew he was the office freak, and he didn't want any part of team building, especially if it meant being paired off with someone who would chat his ear off the entire time they were hiking.

He blew out a breath and opened the email.

Flashlights. Spare batteries. Smartwool hiking socks. How could wool be smart? Hiking boots. Long underwear? In October? Dammit. He was going to have to go shopping. He looked at the calendar. He could totally still get two-day shipping, but he wouldn't be able to try any of this stuff on. And he *had* to try it on. Which meant—sporting goods stores. Alden's stomach rolled.

It's not that he had anything against fitness. He jogged at the park four days a week, rain or shine. He even did some crunches and pushups every once in a while. But he could order his running gear online and do his crunches naked on the bathroom floor while waiting for the water to warm up. He didn't have to go *out* to *places* where people knew stuff he didn't and then *ask them for help.*

A yellow banner popped up in the lower right corner of his screen.

New message from Kit Taylor. Open?

Goddamn it. Stupid fucker was probably hitting "reply-all" to express his boundless-fucking-enthusiasm for this macho survivalist bullshit.

Alden opened the message.

Hey partner, I'll get enough energy bars for both of us—I get a discount at the health food place next to my gym. Do you have any food allergies?

Glaring at his screen, Alden tried to make sense of the message. Realization hit him like a glass of icy water in the face. Kit Taylor was his assigned partner for the team-building weekend. Kit fucking Taylor.

Lots of people in the office annoyed Alden, but Kit Taylor was at the top of the list. It was bad enough the man was a walking advertisement for an outdoor living catalog, all brawny muscles and thermal henleys under plaid lumberjack shirts, or that he looked like an REI model, even though he was actually a field biologist. No, Kit Taylor was also the kind of guy who volunteered for tough assignments and showed up to team meetings in muddy hiking boots. The kind of guy who probably kept a stockpile of canned goods and artillery in his basement, just in case the apocalypse decided to roll up on him.

The kind of guy who made Alden feel both terrified and inadequate. And somewhere, in his stupid lizard brain, turned on. Kit had a way of looking at him during the weekly all staff meeting that set his blood humming in his ears. It was completely irrational. Alden didn't date. He didn't even hook up. Not unless he counted Tommy, but that would be even more pathetic than just admitting it: He was celibate, for better or for worse, and he was too fucked up to do anything about it.

But if he wasn't? If he actually could tolerate the idea of letting someone past his carefully erected walls? Kit Taylor, with his giant shoulders and his tight shirts and his catalog-model hair, could definitely get it.

Alden hated him for it.

Partners. For their weekend in the woods. He read Kit's email again. He grudgingly had to admit that it was really nice of Kit to ask about the allergies. And to offer to get the discounted energy bars.

No food allergies, he typed back. *Thanks for asking. Why don't I double up on batteries?*

There. Even. Ish. How much did energy bars even cost?

The yellow banner popped up again. Click.

Awesome. This is gonna be epic. I hope you're bringing your "A" game, cause we can totally beat the rest of the team to the summit.

He even typed like a walking macho cliche.

Alden didn't reply.

Kit stared at his computer screen long after it was clear Kaufman wasn't going to answer him again. Alden Kaufman was an enigma. He worked from home, only coming into the office for the weekly team meeting. He was some uber-genius data analyst, and everyone talked about him and his work in awed tones. Whatever. Kaufman wasn't the one out there *gathering* the data. That was for guys like Kit. Guys who could brave the weather, literally and figuratively, outside of an office or lab. So what if Kit wasn't the stereotype of a scientist like Kaufman? He got his job done, and he was damned good at it. His life as an outdoorsman made him ideally suited for fieldwork—he was attentive, respectful, and thorough.

That didn't mean Alden was helpless or anything. Kit had seen him running at the park in the evenings, earbuds in, clipping along at a seven-minute mile pace like running was as easy as breathing. Kit could run, and he could even hit a seven-minute pace for about thirty seconds, but he definitely didn't make it look easy. Alden didn't just make it look easy, he made it look like poetry, his slender body moving in perfect rhythm, blond hair bouncing on his forehead. He looked like a Nike commercial.

But forget getting to know him. Those earbuds. They were *always* in Alden's ears, which made it impossible to hold a conversation with him. Kit had tried a few times to strike one up. He knew very little about Alden. He knew he was gay—common ground was good—and that he had lived in the area all his life, but Kit had eventually given up on trying to chat him up after weeks of grunted one-word answers.

Kit knew where he wasn't wanted. Alden might be cute in a skinny-hipster way, with his dark-rimmed reading glasses and the tattoo curling around his forearm, but he was the very definition of a cold fish. Every time Kit tried to get a good look at the tattoo, Kaufman would tug his sleeves back down and glare at him. Maybe Kit wasn't hip enough to see the tattoo.

Whatever. He didn't need to see Kaufman's tattoos to know he was in shape and would be able to maintain the pace on their three-day hike. That was the important thing. They'd make it to the summit with a minimum of kumbaya-singing, and they'd show that they were capable of communicating and problem-solving. Kit would get assigned to the project Dr. Evans was planning in Costa Rica, Kaufman would put his earbuds back in, and they would go back to ignoring each other.

"Wool can absorb thirty percent of its own weight in water and still feel dry against the skin. Put a little lanolin on them, and your feet will stay warm, dry, and soft as a baby's bottom."

The salesperson at the camping store, whose name tag dubbed him "Brent," looked either bored, stoned, or both as he gave Alden his pitch for the wool hiking socks over the other, machine-made fiber socks that were half the price. Alden cringed internally. Sixty dollars for socks he would wear one weekend and then never again. But he didn't like the idea of cold, wet feet either.

Some pop song came squalling through the speakers of the store's sound system like a drunk kitten. Alden winced and pulled his earbuds from his pocket.

"Look, you seem to be good at your job. If you could just help me find everything on this list, and not actually, you know, talk about it, that would be great." He thrust the list at Brent and shoved his earbuds in his ears. The soothing tones of his brown noise app separated him from the irritating cacophony around him, instantly calming his rapidly fraying nerves. Brent looked at him, shrugged, and started pulling items off the shelves and tossing them into Alden's basket.

The basket got heavy quickly, and Alden was hyperventilating at the total rapidly climbing in his head. Hell, hiking was expensive. When they got to the tents, he nearly bolted. Instead, he took a deep breath, and said "I'll be sleeping alone in it, I'm likely to only use it once, and I want the easiest thing possible to assemble."

Brent nodded and grabbed a tent off the shelf. "You're all set, dude."

Alden took the tent, then made his way to the front of the store to pay for his weekend of hell.

"Five hundred fifty-seven dollars?" He pulled the earbuds out of his ears. "Are you high?"

He immediately regretted his choice of words. But still. *Five hundred fifty-seven dollars.*

The girl behind the counter laughed. "Not at the moment. Hey, you're getting a great discount on the pack. This stuff costs what it costs because it's the best. Most people accumulate it over time, you know? They don't typically buy it all at once. So where are you going?"

Alden glared at her, but she kept smiling. Small talk. Ugh. "My office is doing a team building thing. One of my colleagues and I are going hiking."

"Oh, nice. Where do you work that pays you to hike? That sounds like an awesome perk."

He was pretty sure they didn't share the same definitions of "nice," "awesome," or "perk."

"I'm a civilian data analyst for the Army Corps of Engineers."

"Right on. Go ahead and slide your card." She pointed at the terminal.

"Right."

"Here you go, Mr. Data Analyst. Keep this in case you need to return anything." She folded the receipt and handed it to him. "Have a good time on your work retreat."

A good time. As-fucking-if.

In the car on his way home, he called his mom.

"Alden, honey." Her familiar answer on the second ring made him smile. She never just said hello.

"Hi, Mom. I have some bad news. I can't visit this weekend; I have a work thing."

"Oh, honey." She didn't sound terribly disappointed, which stung a bit. "That's okay, you should be out there living your life."

"It's just a stupid team-building exercise. Hiking with one of the field researchers on my team. You know I would much rather spend that time with you."

"You should be spending time with young people, Alden. You can't spend every weekend with me—you'll never meet anyone that way."

He could hear her disapproval through the phone line. She wasn't that old, only in her sixties, but since Alden's father had passed away, she tended to act like her life was mostly over. Alden hated that, and he hated that he couldn't make her see that she was still fun to be around, in spite of everything recent years had done to their lives.

"Mom, I like spending time with you. You're my favorite person."

She made a fussy noise. "Well, I don't know nothing. Call me when you get back from your hiking trip."

"I will, Mom. Have a good weekend, okay? Don't let Mr. Hendrick win too many chess games in a row. He gets cocky and then I'll have to take him down a notch next time I visit."

"What makes you think I let him win?"

He smiled. "Because you never let me win, and I always beat him. I love you, Mom."

"I love you too, honey." She disconnected the call.

He hated that she was still holding out hope that he would meet someone and make some sort of normal life out of his solitary existence. She knew how hard it was for him to attempt normalcy, but she *hoped*. And he was so damn tired of disappointing her.

TWO

Kit pulled his Explorer into the parking lot of the lab and put it in park. He expected to be the first one there. He *expected* to have a few moments to enjoy the quiet solitude of five thirty in the morning, a hot cup of coffee, and a couple of still-warm doughnuts—probably the best food he'd get to eat over the next few days. Not that he minded camping food. He'd gotten used to it over the years.

But no.

A blue Prius sat in the parking lot, and bent over its open hatchback was a figure dressed in skinny jeans and a fluorescent green jacket. A figure with a nice, round ass and brand new hiking boots.

Skinny jeans.

He climbed out of the truck, bringing the box of doughnuts with him. "Morning, partner."

Kaufman stood up so quickly, he bumped his head on the hatch. He cringed back away from it, yanking his earbuds out. The look he turned on Kit was one of withering disdain. "I didn't hear you pull up."

"What's going on there?" Kit gestured to the mess all over the inside of the hatchback.

"I bought all this, all this *stuff*, and it won't fit in my fucking pack. And the employees at the camping store were *not* safe people, even though they tried to be pleasant, and I couldn't ask *them* for help, so I thought I'd just get here early and figure it out, but now *you're* here, and..."

"Whoa, buddy, slow down. You're like, speaking in italics and stuff. Here, have a doughnut." He opened the box and held it out.

"A doughnut?" Kaufman's face softened. Apparently, he had a soft spot for sugar. Something they had in common. "You brought doughnuts?"

"Yeah, man. Team building. We're a team. Have a doughnut; I'll help you pack that thing."

Kaufman scowled. Good lord, the man was impossible to please. Kit felt sorry for the employees at the camping store. Hopefully they got a good commission for selling him all this stuff.

Kit waved the box around. "What, don't tell me you don't like doughnuts."

"I don't—" Kaufman's shoulders slumped and he sucked in a breath. Possibly the first one he'd taken since Kit got out of the car. "I *like* doughnuts. Thank you for bringing doughnuts. It was a real nice thing to do." He pulled hand sanitizer out of his coat pocket, rubbed it on his hands, and he actually took a doughnut.

Kit left the box sitting on the hood of the Explorer, hoping the still-running engine would keep it warm.

"Let's see what we're working with." He unzipped the front of the pack. Empty. He shoved the sleeping bag in first. "What are you planning to sleep in?"

"The long underwear." Kaufman's words were slurred, his mouth full of doughnut.

Kit rolled up the garments and shoved them close to the sleeping bag. "You got a bear can for this food?"

"What's a bear can?"

"A good fucking idea is what it is. Bears are smart. They want your food. You think your backpack zipper is going to keep them out?"

"I didn't even know there were bears, for fuck's sake. I mean, I know there are bears in the Smokies, but you don't expect to actually see them." Kaufman's forehead wrinkled up. "Do you think we'll really see bears?"

"They aren't exactly mythological creatures or anything, and we're going hiking in their house." Kit muttered, trying to remind himself that this was new to Alden. "Okay, that's okay. There's a little bit more room in mine. Enough for some of the food. We'll eat what we can't fit in it tonight. You can share my deodorant and toothpaste."

"I'm not sharing your deodorant."

"Fine, get sweaty and stinky and smell yourself for three days. I don't care." Kit liked to think of himself as an easy-going guy, but Kaufman was going to be on his very last nerve before they even finished packing his backpack. Why had he asked Dr. Evans to pair them up again? Right, seven-minute miles. "I brought a camping stove, so we can leave yours here." Kit put the water in the pack and started loading clothing and other soft items around it.

"Only three pairs of socks?"

"They're twenty dollars a pair."

"Well, at least you got good socks. You'll be glad of that when they're soaking wet and you have nothing to change into."

"I can't believe they didn't cancel the trip." Kaufman scowled. "The weather is going to be terrible."

"It wouldn't be much of a team-building exercise if they

canceled it over a little cold rain. Besides, it's supposed to stay north of us, up in Kentucky and West Virginia. We'll be fine."

There, Kaufman's pack was loaded as well as Kit could load it.

"Here. Try it on, let me adjust the straps for you."

"I don't need—"

"Dude. Come on, no fronting. The tag from the store is still attached. You've never used this thing before."

"Who the fuck says things like 'no fronting'?" Kaufman grumbled as he slipped his arms through the shoulder straps. "What does that even mean?"

"Hey, just because I know more f-words than you do..." Kit let that trail off as he checked the straps. When he stuck his hand in between Kaufman's back and the pack to see how much room there was, Kaufman sucked in a sharp breath. *Interesting.* He walked around Kaufman more slowly now, checking a strap here, adjusting the fit there, letting his hands linger slightly at Kaufman's slender waist. For a split second, he had the crazy urge to slide his hands up under Kaufman's shirt and see what else made him gasp.

"For fuck's sake Kit, stop groping me and get on with it. Are you done?"

Kit pulled his hands back like he'd been burned. *Bad idea.* "Yeah. I'm done. If that starts rubbing anywhere, let me know and we'll adjust it."

"Thank you." Kaufman practically mumbled the words.

"You're welcome." He smiled cheerfully, even though confused embarrassment still coursed through his veins. "Still got about fifteen before anyone else shows up. Wanna help me finish off those doughnuts?"

Alden shrugged back out of the pack and set it down next to the car. "Sure, thank you."

They ate the doughnuts in silence, mostly. To Kit's surprise, Alden broke the silence first.

"I'm not good with people under the best circumstances, and I was flustered when you got here. I appreciate your help, and I'm sorry if I came across as a dick."

The apology went a long way toward burning off some of Kit's annoyance, though it did absolutely nothing to quench his inappropriate fascination with Alden. "A little bit of a dick. But that's okay. I can take it."

He picked up the empty doughnut box and carried it across the parking lot to the trash can. When he turned back, three more cars were pulling into the lot. He greeted the rest of the team with a wave and returned to Alden's side. Alden offered him a rare, shaky smile, placing the earbuds back in his ears. As they climbed into the Explorer to head to the trail a few minutes later, Kit realized that was the longest he'd ever seen Alden without them.

"So why do you have such a bug up your ass about this weekend?"

Alden looked up at Kit in surprise. They'd been on the road half an hour, and so far, Kit had seemed content with the silence.

"I don't have anything up my ass. I don't like hiking. I think extreme team-building is stupid, and I don't think either of us will be better at our jobs because we bonded over campfire stories."

Kit frowned. "But...you're getting paid to do something other people do for fun. You can appreciate that, right?"

Alden tried his most patient explaining voice.

"I'm salaried. So are you. It's not like we get a bonus for this.

Basically, we're giving up a weekend we could be doing our typical restful weekend things in order to be uncomfortable in each other's company."

"Typical restful weekend things?" Kit laughed. "What do you do on the weekends, Kaufman?"

"My name is Alden."

"Alden. What's your deal? You go out to the club? Get your dance on?" Kit started making obnoxious *oontz-oontz-oontz* noises with his mouth and drumming on the steering wheel. Alden got a sudden mental image of Kit in a dance club, lights flashing, one of those inexplicably tight thermal henleys clinging to his sweaty skin. His hair would be damp and the men would be—well. They'd be all over him, wouldn't they? Kit was, frankly, ridiculously hot. They wouldn't be able to resist touching him with their hands, their mouths. Rubbing themselves on his round, muscled ass. And Kit seemed like the kind of guy who would get lost in the moment, leaning into the touches and grinding with the music.

Alden could practically feel those hands and mouths, those hard bodies against his own. He'd be helpless, crowded, *terrified*. And still, thinking about it being not him but *Kit* receiving the attention gave him a weird boner. "Stop that. No. I visit my mom. I watch TV. I read. I run. Why, what do you do?"

Kit gave him a funny look. "I go hiking."

Alden laughed. "No, for real."

"For real. I go hiking, camping, fishing. I love it."

"That's why you do field work—this is *fun* to you."

"Yeah. I love my job. I know guys like you who spend your time in spreadsheets don't see the joy in getting out in nature and observing firsthand, but so much science happens because guys like me go out and look at the world. We take its measure for you."

Stung, Alden defended himself. "I'm a real scientist too. I

make observations and look for larger patterns in data collected from multiple sources. Not just your samples and your notes, but historical data and measurements from other organizations."

"Hey, everyone on the team respects your insights, but I wouldn't be happy doing your job. Just like you wouldn't be happy doing mine."

Alden let that thought sink in for a while, laying his head against the window and enjoying the cold against his skin. Was *he* happy doing his job? It certainly wasn't what he'd expected to be doing with his life. Spending his days at a desk with the shades drawn tightly closed to isolate him from a world that proved too much for him more often than not. No, he used to imagine doing fieldwork himself—out on a boat or along a shoreline, salt in the air and on his skin. He used to imagine being another kind of man altogether. It used to be a possibility.

"Where's your mom live?" Kit's voice cut through his thoughts. "That you go visit her on the weekends?"

"Oh, um, she lives in a community for disabled adults with limited mobility. She uses a wheelchair sometimes, and she struggles with her medication schedules. She's diabetic, and she can get really sick really quickly if her sugars aren't right."

"I'm sorry."

Alden shrugged. There was a big raw place inside of him when he thought about everything he *couldn't* do for his mom, which of course made him think of the things he couldn't even do for himself. And then he felt guilty because once again, he was making it all about himself. But that's who he was now, for better or for worse.

"She's better off there than with a jerk like me."

Kit got quiet then, and Alden put his earbuds in. He didn't need Kit looking at him like some bonus kind of fieldwork. He wasn't here to be observed. He just needed to survive this weekend, and then everything could go back to normal. Not that *his* life was normal. Everything could go back to routine. His routine. His nice, *safe* routine.

Kit looked over at Alden, all turned in on himself. Those ever-present earbuds were back in his ears, his eyes were closed, and his pretty mouth had gone tight and shaky. He was pretending to be asleep.

She's better off there than with a jerk like me.

If it hurt Kit to hear those words, how much had it hurt Alden to say them?

And why did it matter to Kit? The guy *was* a jerk. Close-minded, uptight, snobby. He was an asshole.

And a great big question mark.

He'd blushed bright red when Kit had joked about dancing. What had he been thinking about? Remembering some particular dance-club escapade?

Kit tried to picture Alden dancing. His svelte, twinky frame would attract a certain attention, and that chilled disdain would attract another kind. Alden could have his pick of men at any club Kit ever went to. But try as he might, Kit couldn't picture Alden relaxing enough to get into the pickup scene. Not that Kit was part of that scene either. He'd never liked the loud noise or the weird energy in the eyes of certain guys who had to get wasted to hook up with other men. The sex...well, that he liked. He liked those moments of intimacy that turned a stranger into someone dear, at least for as long as it took them both to get off. He didn't mind a rough shove against a wall, or a blowjob in the backseat of a car. That kind of sex was easy, fun. And once the guys weren't strangers anymore? He'd had a few regular fuck buddies, but over the years, they all got into real relationships and stopped having no-strings sex with the guy who spent months at a time out in the woods with high tech cameras and recording devices. In the age of big fat gay weddings and flash-mob proposals, no one seemed to want an absentee boyfriend. It was easier to keep it casual, to not get so close that he put himself in the position of choosing between his work and a lover.

Damn. Now he was getting maudlin.

He saw a sign for a Starbucks at an upcoming exit and tapped Alden on the shoulder.

Alden jerked upright, his blond hair falling in his eyes for just a moment before he brushed it away. For a split second, he looked terrified, then his armor swung into place, and he raised an eyebrow.

"Starbucks at the next exit. Yes? No?"

"God, yes." Alden whispered fervently. "And let me buy—since you brought doughnuts."

Kit laughed. "Okay, but I'm warning you, I'm going to order the biggest, froufrouiest thing they've got."

"Of course you are." Alden rolled his eyes. "And you're macho enough you can do that without ever worrying about it messing with your tough guy image."

Bemused, Kit asked "You're so worried about your tough guy image you let it dictate what you order at Starbucks?"

"No. That would require actually having a tough guy image. I'm a nerdy, queer, agoraphobic scientist. I have literally no game." But his lips turned up in a smile. The little fucker was self-deprecating.

"You got a little game." Kit held up his thumb and his forefinger about an inch apart. "Maybe that much?"

Now Alden laughed out loud, and Kit felt a warmth stirring in him. Alden's face transformed completely when he laughed. The distrust and petulance disappeared, and something sweet, almost innocent took over. It made Kit want to give him a hug. Or touch his dick. Maybe the guy wasn't so bad. *Maybe you're just horny and like it when guys laugh at your jokes.*

And that thought led down a dangerous road. He wasn't here to make moon-eyes at the office asshole, no matter what his libido thought. They'd get to the summit, get back, and go their separate ways.

THREE

Despite the stop at Starbucks—which Alden desperately needed—they made it to the trail head by nine. Kit was an unsettlingly pleasant traveling partner. He kept the music—a playlist of some kind of folksy alt-pop that was as agreeable as it gets—low and didn't try to talk too much after the Starbucks stop, which should have been perfect, but now that Alden was caffeinated, he found he might not have minded the talking so much.

His first impression of Kit—before he'd ever met him face to face and realized how freakishly good-looking the man was—had been that he was friendly and enthusiastic like a Labrador puppy. But their brief conversations had him thinking that wasn't quite right—Kit was as serious as Alden was about what they did. He was defensive about his credentials, which were as good as Alden's own, and passionate about his work. Alden liked that. He didn't mind Labrador puppies either.

"Where's everyone else?" he asked, glancing around.

"They're taking the other trail." Kit scowled at the clouds forming overhead. "They both converge at the same point, but they go around opposite sides of the mountain. The terrain of this one is the most technical."

Right, so of course they were the only team to choose it over the other, more leisurely hikes. Fine.

"Who goes first?" He asked as they shouldered their packs and approached the trail head, trying to find his own inner Labrador so he could muster some of the enthusiasm that came naturally to Kit.

"Much as I appreciate the way you look in those skinny jeans, I think I should probably go first since I'm more familiar with hiking." Kit grinned.

Alden swallowed hard. The last thing he needed was Kit turning all that enthusiasm to flirting. Because now Alden was going to be looking at Kit's ass. Not that Kit wore skinny jeans. No, *he* wore some kind of mountain-man work pants covered in pockets. Probably something he wore when he was out doing field work. They were not unsexy, not exactly, but they were a far cry from anything Alden would have chosen to appeal to another man. And yet he was pretty sure he'd be seeing them in his dirtiest dreams for weeks to come. Kit wasn't just unsettlingly pleasant; he was straight up unsettling. His large, competent hands on Alden's body earlier as he'd adjusted the straps on the backpack had felt so good, and Alden's reaction to those hands had been far stronger than was strictly comfortable. He'd been overwhelmed with the desire to touch back, to take the measure of Kit's wide shoulders with his hands, to feel the strength in that chest and those muscular thighs. And now he was *flirting*. God help them both.

Kit set a brisk pace, but nothing Alden would have trouble maintaining.

"I've seen you at the park," Kit called over his shoulder. "You keep a pretty good clip when you're running. I figured we could cover a lot of ground this first day, in case you're sore tomorrow and we have to slow down."

Alden flinched. "I can handle it."

"You use different muscles when you're hiking than when you're running."

"I said I can handle it."

"Great. Let's pick it up then." Kit started hiking faster, his long legs carrying him quickly. Alden had to practically jog to keep up. Kit was clearly either super competitive or a sadist. Well, that was okay with Alden—friendly competition could be fun. Maybe hiking wouldn't be like the track meets in high school, where Alden had dominated the distance events but competition always propelled him to be better. He took a deep breath and pushed on, his heart quickening as he lengthened his stride and leaned forward. Kit could move, that was for sure, but Alden could too. And he wasn't going to give Kit the satisfaction of leaving him behind.

Things had been going so well back in the car, but by the time they stopped to eat, Alden had completely withdrawn back into his shell, grunting one-word answers when Kit asked him how he was enjoying the hike. So, Kit stopped asking. But then Alden reached for his earbuds, and Kit put a hand on his arm.

"Don't."

Alden pulled his hand away and his blue-gray eyes widened. "Excuse me?"

Kit knew he was being a jerk about the earbuds. Obviously, Alden got something out of whatever he listened to beyond just enjoyment. But Kit didn't care what Alden was getting out of it right now. He needed Alden to be present.

"You need to be alert and aware of your surroundings. This isn't like walking around a city."

Alden rolled his eyes. "I'm sure you're alert and aware enough for both of us."

"Team-building. How much of a team can we possibly be if I'm doing all the work?"

"Wasn't that your plan anyway?" Alden got right up in his face, intense and quivering. "To get us up the mountain as quickly as possible and then go our separate ways? That's why you're practically sprinting? Trying to leave me in your dust? You got paired with me, and that sucks, but I'm trying my best not to be a burden."

Kit shook his head. "I fucking requested you, dumbass."

"*Dumbass*?" Alden practically screeched. "I am the best goddamn data analyst in the Southeast." He stilled as the rest of Kit's sentence penetrated his attitude. "Wait—did you say—you requested me?"

Kit looked down at his feet. He hadn't anticipated having to come clean like this. "Yeah. You're a runner, and you're pretty quiet. I figured it would be an easy hike for you. And yeah, I thought it would be good to get to know you. We're the only queer people out at work, and sometimes it's just nice to be around someone you can relax around and not wait for the other shoe to fall and find out they're secretly a bigot. But I get it, you don't want to be friends. You seem to get a rise out of being a dick. We don't have to like each other."

Alden glared at him for a long moment, and the longer he stared, the smaller Kit felt. And that was fucking ridiculous, because out of the two of them, he was the one who knew what he was doing.

Finally, Alden shrugged and said, "I like dick better than dumbass."

"Yeah? It suits you." And apparently, Kit was going to sink to his level.

"I won't use the earbuds when we're hiking." Alden conceded. "But I might need them some of the other times. They help with my anxiety."

Kit could live with that. "Are you done with your lunch?" He held open the ZipLoc bag he used for trash, and Alden stuffed his inside.

After securing the trash, Kit gestured up trail. "There's a waterfall about four miles further up, and there are campsites nearby there. It would be a good place to stop for the night."

Alden squinted up the trail. "Okay. Lead the way."

Kit eased back on the pace after that, and stopped every once in a while to point things out that he figured Alden would miss otherwise. At one point, Alden stopped him with a hand on his shoulder. When he looked back, Alden was pointing, wide-eyed, at a beaver dam on the creek down below, two large, flat-tailed beavers crawling all over it. His obvious delight was infectious.

"I've never seen one before," he whispered, "I mean, not in person."

"They're very resourceful," Kit whispered back, watching Alden going all soft over the creatures. "And as big as a dog. They don't usually come out much during the day."

"Why are we whispering?" Alden looked away from the dam and met Kit's gaze. "I started it didn't I?"

Laughing, Kit nodded. "You like animals."

"I do." Alden smiled. "All kinds, but I thought, when I was a kid, I'd be a marine biologist. I wanted to study dolphins and whales."

"And you grew up to analyze habitat damage in the Great Smokies. Which, by the way, is really important work. I'm glad you're the one doing it."

"Well, the world looks different on paper." Alden started up the trail again, and this time, Kit followed. "I didn't want to move away from home to go to the coast somewhere."

"Because of the agoraphobia?"

"No. I wasn't agoraphobic when I was younger. That came later. I told you my mom is diabetic and has a bunch of comorbid conditions. Since it's dangerous for her to live alone, I wanted to stay close to her so I could help her. Not that I did much good. After she lost part of her leg three years ago, we retrofitted the house for her wheelchair, but in the end, she needed more help than I could give her."

"What about your dad? Is he not in the picture?"

Alden went stock still, and his eyes got huge. "He didn't do her much good either. He—" Alden paused, shook his head. "—He passed away when I was in grad school."

"I'm sorry."

Alden shrugged, one of those flinching, uncomfortable movements he usually made before he snapped out an f-bomb. Kit was sure that shrug was supposed to be casual, unaffected, but the jerky, tortured way Alden's body twitched suggested it was anything but. Before Kit could ask, Alden changed the subject. "What about you? Is your family around?"

"My family lives in Tennessee, on the other side of the mountains. Mom teaches third grade. Dad is a judge. I have an older sister—Kelly—who married a lawyer and stays home with her two little girls. Abigail is six and Zoey is three. I kinda like being Uncle Kit."

"Do they know you're gay?" There was something wistful in Alden's voice. He stopped and looked at Kit.

"Yeah." Kit nodded, remembering his awkward conversation with his parents when he came out. "It was weird for a few months. Mom kept asking if I was sure. But that was years ago. Now they just keep waiting for me to meet 'the one' and get partnered up."

"That must be nice. I wish it was like that for me."

They started walking again as Kit digested that. It didn't seem right. Alden was out at work of all places, but not to his family? "You're in the closet? Really? How old are you?"

"Haha." Alden deadpanned as he stopped and turned back to Kit. "No, I'm not in the closet. I came out as a teenager. My mom loves me but—sometimes I think the reality of me makes her uncomfortable. Denial ain't just a river in Egypt."

"Dude, for real?" The more Kit learned about Alden's life, the more the aggressive defensiveness made sense.

"I couldn't make this shit up. It's not like she's mean about it, she's just Southern. And when she was growing up, people didn't talk about homosexuality in her household. My aunt is much worse. Anyway, your family. They sound like nice people."

"They are nice people." Kit smiled. "Maybe you'll meet them someday."

Alden went still, eyes wide, then he flushed. "Right. That's totally going to happen."

Kit had obviously stepped on another of Alden's landmines. "I'm just making small talk, Kaufman."

"Well, I'm really bad at small talk, can we—?" Alden waved his hand in a vague forward gesture.

Kit nodded. "Yeah. If you need some earbud time, I'll keep an ear out."

With a bitter little smile, Alden patted the pocket of his jacket like a smoker feeling for his cigarettes. "I'm okay. Thanks, though."

They moved up the mountain silently after that, which was a relief. Kit felt freed from the obligation of making conversation, which normally came easily, but not with Alden. Most conversations were straightforward, relying on social cues to smooth over any awkwardness. But there was no clear trail in a conversation with Alden. The path was littered with obstacles, and Kit could never tell how big or treacherous the obstacle was going to be. Why certain subjects seemed to irritate Alden, and others seemed to flat out devastate him.

As they walked, Kit tried to let that go. He didn't understand Alden, and that was okay. They could enjoy each other's company without talking. At least, he thought *he* enjoyed Alden's company. He wasn't sure that was mutual.

When they reached the falls, he heard Alden's breath catch behind him, and he turned, a grin spreading on his face. Finally, something had gotten through to his prickly hiking partner.

"Isn't it gorgeous? I usually come at it from the other side—" He pointed across the river to a rock outcropping overlooking the falls. "—that spot there is great for selfies."

"I came here once when I was kid." Alden's eyes were huge. "With my dad. I just felt the strongest memory of his hand on my shoulder." His voice was thin and soft, barely more than a whisper, but Kit heard every syllable as if they were etching themselves into his own memory. "That was the day I fell in love with water. The way it moves, the way it sings." Alden closed his eyes and spread out his arms wide. "Peace."

Kit smiled but didn't say anything. It was enough to watch and enjoy Alden's moment. Alden's peace. After a moment, he shook himself, opened his eyes, and smiled back at Kit. "Thank you."

"For what?"

Alden shrugged, not one of his twitchy, defensive shrugs, but a softer moment. "For letting me have this. Or for giving it to me? I'm not sure. But I appreciate it."

Kit swallowed thickly. "Of course, I mean, you're welcome. Should we go find a campsite?"

Alden nodded, his eyes huge. "Not too far from here? I'd love it if we could hear the falls."

"Let's see what we can find."

Thanks to the rain that threatened, they had their pick of two campsites near the falls. One even had a view down the mountain to the west. Sure, the clouds would probably keep the sunset mellow, but maybe they'd get lucky.

"This one?" He gestured to the site. "Looks nice to me, what do you think?"

Alden glanced over his shoulder in the direction of the other site, then gave another jerky shrug. "I'll take your word for it."

FOUR

"I need to take my meds; do you remember which pocket you put them in?" Alden had checked all the ones he could see on the outside of the pack but hadn't found them yet. He was sure he'd grabbed the bottles from the medicine cabinet this morning and meted out enough for three days. His pill case had been with him while they were packing. "Are they in that bear thing?"

"Meds?" Kit went still. "I didn't do anything with your meds."

"What do you mean? You packed my goddamn bag. They were right there, with the camping stove and the—" The first bite of panic was like swallowing an ice cube whole. It seemed to lodge in his throat and choke his voice from him.

"I mean exactly what I said—I didn't ever see your meds. I didn't pack your stove because we had mine. I must have overlooked them." There was almost an apology in Kit's voice, but Alden was still blinking and trying not to vomit.

"I need..." *I need to not hyperventilate in front of Kit. I need to take a deep breath. I need—*

"Whoa—calm down." Kit's hands came down on Alden's shoulders. "Sit here." He lowered Alden down to the log next to the fire and pushed his head down between his knees. "What kind of meds are they? What's going to happen if you can't take them for a few days?"

"I'll go out of my goddamn mind with panic is what'll happen." Alden snapped, sitting upright and shoving Kit's hand away. "I take an SSRI nightly, and Xanax for acute anxiety."

"Okay. How can we keep that from happening? Are there special meditations? Breathing exercises? Because either direction, we're at least a day's hike from a trail head."

Alden took a deep breath and tried to concentrate on what Kit was saying rather the panic trying to get a grip on his brain. *I'm safe. I'm safe with Kit.*

"I don't know what will happen if I miss the anti-depressants." The thought sent another stab of fear through him, but the more he talked, the smaller the ice cube in his chest seemed to feel. "I need to feel safe, or I'm more likely to have a panic attack. The thought of missing my meds for two days makes me feel uncertain about what my body and brain are going to go through, which makes me feel unsafe, which triggers a panic spiral."

"How can I help?"

"Talking to me like this helps, but I'd feel better if you were sitting down and not towering over me like a giant."

Kit sat, right on the hard ground in front of Alden. "I'm sorry. I didn't see them, or I would have packed them. I—God, Alden, I feel like an ass."

He looked sorry, too. Gone was the affable catalogue-model smile. He looked—he looked like Alden felt. Uncertain and ashamed.

"Talk to me." Alden said. "Tell me why you love camping. Maybe hearing the good things about it will help."

"You got room on that log for me?"

Alden scooted sideways, and Kit sat next to him, his big

warm body a solid wall of heat and comfort. If he tried, Alden could hear the rush of water from the falls. His shoulders relaxed incrementally, and he let out a soft sigh. This could work. "Tell me, please?"

"I started camping with my dad when I was just a little kid. I did Boy Scouts, too. It was something that was always fascinating to me, being outdoors, out in the world—being around people didn't feel like being in the world to me." Kit's face held a faraway expression. "Out here, out in nature, everything moves, but there's a stillness to everything that you don't get when you're in society. People aren't still. They can be stagnant, but there's a sourness to that."

"You have the soul of a poet," Alden observed drily. He meant it as a compliment, but Kit's face tightened up into a scowl.

"Don't make fun. You asked."

"And you're trying to talk all pretty to impress me?" Alden leaned into Kit's warmth, knocking their knees together.

"I'm trying to talk all pretty because words aren't adequate to the way I feel when I close my eyes and go to sleep with the sounds of the world in my ears."

"Society makes me feel trapped," Alden admitted, his voice barely more than a whisper. "It's a big part of why I try to stay home."

"I always thought agoraphobia means you can't leave your house?"

Alden shook his head. "That's only in very extreme cases. I would prefer to stay in a controlled environment as much as possible, but I do leave my house. Obviously." He gestured to the woods and sky. "I'm in the *world,* now."

"Obviously."

Something in Kit's expression, the way his eyebrows knit together, the way his lips held a slightly bemused smile, told

Alden that there was nothing obvious about it at all. But how could he explain how his brain worked to someone who was as easy-going and uninhibited?

"I'm really not the way people stereotypically think of agora-phobes. Leaving the house isn't what scares me. I just... I get panic attacks in public places. And even if I don't have a full-on attack, the anxiety puts me on edge."

Nodding thoughtfully, Kit replied, "I've noticed your edges. Go on."

"I'm not a nice person when I'm on edge. I snap at people, say rude things. I usually regret them later, but the idea of apol-ogizing sends me into a shame-panic spiral, so I let them think I'm just that big of a prick."

Kit laughed. "You're like a caged animal, snapping at anyone who tries to open the door."

"And you think that's funny?" Alden had to admit, the comparison was apt, but it stung a little that Kit found it amusing.

"No, I don't actually. I was laughing at myself, and how often I've been completely puzzled by how you reply when I try to be nice to you. I thought you hated me. What do the meds do?"

Alden cleared his throat, blushing. "They take some of the edges off. They make it so I can concentrate on my work without worrying for days in advance about my weekly trip to the grocery store or talking to the gate attendant where mom lives."

"What makes you feel safe?"

"My house. My brown noise app. Running. Anything that separates me out and away from the things that trigger my anxi-ety. Right now, you."

"Yeah?" The catalogue-model smile was back, and this time it was directed at Alden. Wow, no one had ever smiled at him quite like that before—the sweetness of it sent a wave of confused longing through him.

"That's actually kind of nice," Kit said. "Especially since I'm the one who fucked up. I'm really sorry I didn't see your meds when I was packing."

Grimacing, Alden stood up, turning to hide his flustered reaction to Kit's smile. "Well, you'll be sorrier tomorrow when my brain starts clicking and I have a panic attack. Should we set up our tents?"

"About that. There's only one tent pad at this campsite, and it's not big enough for two tents. I don't mind sharing, but if it makes you feel awkward—" It was Kit's turn to grimace. "—Or unsafe—"

Oh God. Would he even be able to sleep next to someone else? How long had it been? The ice in his chest was back.

"Hey, I'll be in my sleeping bag; you'll be in yours." Kit smiled. "I promise I won't grope you in the night."

A flash of heat and desire swept through Alden's body out of nowhere. He hadn't shared a bed with anyone else in years, and the image of Kit's large hands on his body was as tempting and confusing as the smile had been. "Maybe I can sleep outside."

"Don't be a dork—it's supposed to rain tonight. Here, help me set up the tent."

And then Alden found himself snapping together tent poles and trying not to laugh as Kit made innuendo-laden jokes about poles and sleeves. Even though he'd been upset at being paired with Kit to begin with, he was starting to—God, was he actually starting to like the guy? *Oh no no no no. Bad hormones.* He had worked too hard for too long to keep the guy at arm's length; he could *not* be developing a crush on his coworker.

There was no room for a guy like Kit in Alden's small world, and it had nothing to do with the size of his body or the brightness of his smile, and everything to do with how terrible it would be to let him in, only to find the world even smaller when Kit inevitably moved on.

Kit moved around the campsite, making sure the fire was safely extinguished and the bear can was stashed where it couldn't easily be rolled back down the trail. He glanced toward the tent, watching Alden's graceful silhouette through the walls. Reluctance to intrude swept over him—but he'd put off joining Alden in the tent as long as he could.

When Kit opened the flap to the tent and crawled inside, Alden was sitting on his sleeping bag in long underwear bottoms with his shirt in his lap, feeling around his back with one hand. *Oh, hell.* Kit paused, taking in the sight of all that pale skin and the black tattoos. An octopus perched on one shoulder, tentacles trailing most of the way to the elbow; an anchor sank down the opposite forearm. Alden's body was lean and wiry, as beautiful by lantern light as Kit might have imagined. He was caught by a visceral urge to run his hands over all that skin, to make Alden arch, to make him squirm. Suddenly, sleeping in the same tent and not touching seemed like a really stupid idea.

Alden, of course, was completely oblivious to the effect he was having on Kit.

"Is there—can you look at this a minute?" He turned his back to Kit and pointed awkwardly toward the center of it. "What's going on there?"

The skin over three of Alden's vertebrae was red and raw, with dull yellow welts that would be an angry scabbed red tomorrow. Kit winced. "Chafing. Probably from your pack. Here, I'll put some Neosporin on it." He dug the first aid kit out of his pack and produced the tube and a few Band-Aids. Could Alden see his fingers shaking? He hoped not.

When he touched Alden's back, goose bumps broke out across the skin.

"Your hands are cold."

"Sorry." He applied a thin layer of the ointment on the chafed skin, then capped the tube. Hands still shaking, he peeled the Band-Aids one by one from their wrappers and placed them over the sores. "That should help it heal. In the morning, I've got some stuff in the bear canister that'll help prevent more, if you have any other spots that are rubbing."

"Just my balls," Alden grumbled, pulling on his night shirt. "You could warn a guy."

Kit swallowed, then tried for levity. "I'm not putting Neosporin on your balls."

Alden arched an eyebrow. "I didn't ask you to." Then he crawled into his sleeping bag and turned his back to Kit.

"I like your tattoos," Kit blurted, crawling into his own sleeping bag. There was a long moment of silence, and he wondered if Alden had fallen asleep so quickly.

"Thank you," Alden finally said, and he rolled back over so they were face to face. "I'm not used to other people seeing them."

"Why anchors and octopodes?"

Alden's expression went far away. "Sentimentality. I may not be a marine biologist, but I still love the ocean."

More that they had in common.

"Me too. I've applied for a position with this project in Costa Rica this winter. We've got the grant funding, and the Costa Rican Government has approved all the bureaucratic and diplomatic stuff, but they haven't decided who's going yet."

"You're not—" Alden's eyes went wide. "I guess fieldwork in your own back yard gets boring after a while for a guy like you."

"It's not that—I love these mountains. I just want to see more of the world, you know?"

Alden's lips twisted bitterly. "Not really. But I can see how that appeals to you. I hope you get the position. Goodnight, Kit, would you turn off the lantern?"

He rolled back over.

Kit stared at the curve of Alden's shoulder. Had he done something wrong? Or said something wrong? He flopped onto his back and switched the lantern off, plunging the tent into darkness.

Who was Alden Kaufman? Before this morning, Kit had thought he knew. The man looked like an elegant hipster and cussed like a grumpy sailor, but there was something fragile— no, *brittle*—about him that made Kit want to wrap him up and coddle him like some precious sample collected in the field.

Alden Kaufman, *homo sapiens*. Who knew?

FIVE

Alden woke up to the sound of rain falling on the tent. He had to pee, but it was still dark outside. He tugged on his hiking boots and felt around for the lantern, finding it by the tent flap. The rain, running off the rain cover, hit the back of his head with a thick splat as he crawled out of the tent. Outside the tent, the world was pitch black, but Alden could hear the waterfall, rushing wildly off to his left. The sound was pure and calming, but made his bladder situation that much more urgent. He held the lantern up and picked his way out of the clearing and into the woods.

A few minutes later, he returned to the tent to find Kit sprawled everywhere. Well, he probably wasn't used to sharing his tent, was he? Alden felt around for the zipper of his sleeping bag, then slipped inside. Kit rolled over, making a big snuffling sound, and buried his face in the side of Alden's neck.

Alden froze.

Kit's breath was moist against sensitive skin and hot, a direct contrast to the cool air outside.

"Mmm, you feel good." Kit mumbled, dragging Alden's body close. Then he started snoring.

Oh my God. I have two hundred fifty pounds of mountain man snoring *on me.*

His heart pounded as he held his breath and tried not to laugh. Laughing would wake Kit up, and damn, Kit's body was warm. It was also gorgeous—and Alden wasn't immune to that, no matter how averse he was to romantic entanglements. Apparently, Kit liked to cuddle—and it felt sublime. Alden let out the breath slowly, forcing himself to relax. He didn't mind the cuddling, though he'd never admit it in the morning. It had been a long time since he'd been held like this. Not since he'd shared a shitty apartment in Chapel Hill with Tommy Nguyen during grad school. And Tommy, the touchstone by which Alden judged all other men, had never been as sweetly comforting as Kit. Not that Alden was in much need of comfort back then. The world had been a softer place, and he had taken up more room in it. With Tommy by his side, the possibilities had seemed endless. Until they weren't anymore. Tommy's dry, teasing wit and cheerful camaraderie had been enough to build a relationship but not to sustain one when Alden needed more.

Alden turned toward Kit, pillowing his head on Kit's arm. If he was going to be snored on, he might as well enjoy the silver lining. He was only human, and he craved contact as much as the next person. He could assuage the skin hunger in Kit's slumbering embrace, and maybe it would sustain him in solitude when they parted ways.

Kit woke up with a trickle of water running down the back of his head, and his body pressed up against another body. *Alden.* Somehow, in the middle of the night, he had wrapped himself around his tent mate while they were sleeping. And he had rolled until his back was pressed to the side of the tent, messing up the rain displacement until some of it ended up on him. Fucking wonderful.

At least Alden was dry, and he wouldn't have to listen to the guy bitch about the cold and wet when he woke up.

Kit glanced down at the man sleeping in his arms. His blond hair flopped over Kit's biceps, and his left hand was balled into a loose fist against Kit's chest. Eyelashes—long, but pale like corn-silk—fanned out over the dark circles under his eyes. As Kit watched, Alden's lips twitched, then he started snoring. Kit's fingers itched with the desire to run his hands over the sleek muscles of Alden's arms. He *wanted.*

Inside his sleeping bag, Kit's dick was roaring to life, going from every-morning chub to full on "Let's get some."

Hysterical laughter bubbled up in Kit, and he bit it back, somehow knowing Alden would be pissed if he woke up to Kit laughing.

Ah, but what it would be like, if they were friends like that? The kind of friends who fucked sometimes? What if he could wake Alden up with some kissing and a slow grind to orgasm? What would Alden's face look like when he came? Would that haunted tension slip away and leave him flushed and soft? A shiver of pleasure danced down Kit's spine.

Alden twitched in Kit's arms, then the fist against his chest was a palm, pressing—no, pushing—Kit away.

"For fuck's sake, Kit, get off me. You could have warned me I'd be sleeping with an octopus."

And now Kit laughed, but he let him go.

"Wanna see my tentacle?"

Alden's shoulders shook with mirth, then he rolled away. "It's still raining?"

Kit nodded. "How are you feeling?"

"It's too soon to tell."

"I didn't realize I'd rolled all over you—"

"You were asleep, forget it. It's no big." Alden blushed as he said it, and something in Kit warmed in response. "What time do you think it is?"

"Maybe seven? It's just barely light out there."

"I never get up this early on weekends." Alden burrowed deeper into his sleeping bag, pulling it up around his shoulders and the lower part of his face. "But I guess we need to get moving."

Kit shrugged. "Sleep a little longer if you want. I'll get some water boiling for coffee."

"How are you going to cook in the rain?"

"I'll set up a tarp for shelter, get the stove going under it. We'll be fine."

"Won't you get wet?"

"We're camping. Getting wet happens."

"And you do this for fun." Alden made a scoffing noise, then yawned.

Kit gathered his clothes. "I'm going to get dressed here in the tent, so you know, avert your eyes if you don't want to see."

Alden's head popped out of the sleeping bag. "Well, don't tease a guy. Get on with it."

A nervous flutter filled Kit's belly, then he saw Alden's sleeping bag shaking. The grumpy fucker was laughing at him. He started laughing too.

"You're an asshole, Kaufman." He pulled his night shirt over his head and reached for his pack.

"You like it."

Kit glanced up in surprise, but Alden's eyes were closed again. Truth be told, he *was* enjoying Alden's morning banter. The playfulness of it reminded him of joking with a lover. He found an Under Armor cold gear shirt in his bag and pulled it over his head.

"I think your muscles have their own muscles," Alden's muffled voice came out of the sleeping bag.

He *was* watching. Kit flexed a little, just for fun. Knowing Alden's eyes were on him made him feel hot all over, hyper aware. He knew he had a nice body—he worked hard, and it showed. He wasn't the type to fill his Instagram with gym selfies, but he'd gotten more than one date from the shirtless pic he used for his hook up app profiles. He shimmied out of his sleeping bag and peeled off the long underwear he slept in, trading it for his favorite well-worn pair of Carhartt's.

Across the tent, Alden sighed. "Genetics are so unfair."

Kit chuckled. "Yours have been pretty kind to you too, sasshole."

"Sasshole?" Alden's sleeping bag shook again. "So far I've been a dumbass, a dick, a dickhead, an asshole, and now a 'sasshole.' You're getting more creative with your insults. I like it."

Kit didn't miss how Alden dodged the compliment. Probably for the best. This sort of back and forth definitely wasn't what their boss had in mind for their team building exercise. It was a little too close to straight-up flirting. And no matter what Kit fantasized about in that first-waking haze, he and Alden had no place being the kinds of friends who flirted, fucked, or anything else. Alden was complicated, and Kit didn't do complicated.

———

Alden watched as Kit pulled on a rain jacket and boots and left the tent, then he flopped back on his back and closed his eyes. How the hell was this happening? He wasn't supposed to be *flirting* with Kit fucking Taylor.

But the man had felt *good* wrapped all around him. Alden reached down into his long underwear and squeezed his dick. It was fully hard, and a bead of precome had gathered in the slit.

Just from the proximity to the gorgeous specimen of manhood he happened to be sharing a tent with. Alden preferred to deal with an unwanted erection by jerking off, but what the hell was the protocol for jerking off while camping? He didn't think it would be polite to do it in the tent.

His brain clicked.

Just a fraction of a second, everything went electrified and jerky, and then it was normal again. God, SSRI withdrawal was a bitch.

He gave his cock another gentle tug, then let go. No, he wasn't going to jerk off in the tent. And he wasn't going to ask his coworker if he would mind doing it for him. No matter how good Kit looked with his shirt off.

Sasshole. The nickname made him smile, not just because it suited him—maybe a little too well for comfort—but because Kit had said it in that sweet, teasing voice while paying him a compliment. Not too many people in his life complimented him. Sure, there were accolades at work when he made some connection no one else had made. But a personal compliment? Never. Maybe he didn't deserve them. But it was still nice to hear.

He pulled on his clothes, cold and damp from sitting next to the tent wall. He wished he had jeans that weren't so damned tight. But after spending over five hundred dollars at the camping store the other night, the last thing he needed was to spend money on new jeans too. After paying the assisted living expenses his mother's disability didn't cover every month, his own budget was tight. He was doing better than that shitty student apartment in Chapel Hill—but not by much.

Once he had his boots on, he unzipped the tent, carefully zipping it back to keep the rain *outside*, and went to answer nature's call.

When he returned to the campsite, Kit was pouring boiling water into mugs. "How do you take yours?" he called out.

"Black, please."

Kit nodded. "Go wait in the tent. I'll bring it in."

Alden did as he was told, unzipping the tent flap for Kit when he returned. He took both steaming mugs and held them while Kit joined him.

"The trail looks pretty muddy, and the rain is coming down hard." Kit claimed his mug and took a sip.

"So, what does that mean?" *Brain click.*

"We wait a bit, see if it lets off. We crossed a creek yesterday, which means if we're going to turn back, we have to deal with potential flooding on the trail. I don't know if there's anything the same up ahead, and our cell phones won't work out here to check the maps or hiking forums."

"You've never hiked this trail before?" Alden was surprised; he'd thought Kit knew these woods like the back of his hand.

"Nope. That's why when we were offered our choice of trails yesterday, I picked this one. Plus, it was the longest one. More brownie points."

"Ass-kisser." Alden grunted and took a sip of his coffee.

"So long as it's just rain and not flooding, we can wait it out. We're on high ground here, we have food and water, and we're sheltered from the wind. Enjoy a leisurely cup of instant coffee."

Alden didn't mind not getting up and moving. It felt safe in their little tent, and safe wasn't a feeling he got to enjoy outside of own home very often. "This is pretty good for instant coffee."

Kit raised an eyebrow at him, then passed him the bear can. "Here, have a bar. They aren't bad. The chocolate chip ones are my favorite."

Alden took the canister and poked around inside it. There were two chocolate chip ones; he left those for Kit, taking the blueberry crisp one instead.

"I've never eaten one of these before." He peeled it from the wrapper. "Any warnings?"

"Nah. It's like a granola bar, but not as sweet."

Alden nibbled a bit of the edge. It was dry and thick feeling on his tongue, but when he ignored the texture and concentrated on the flavor, it wasn't bad.

"Well, it's a far cry from chicken soup for breakfast. But it's all right."

"Chicken soup?"

Shit. Alden didn't know how to explain his old post-study rituals with Tommy. "Back when I was in Chapel Hill, I would stay up all night studying with Tommy—my ex—and we'd make chicken soup for breakfast. College kid bullshit. But chicken soup is probably still my ultimate comfort food."

"Mmmm." Kit made an appreciative noise. "Noodles or rice?"

"Definitely rice."

"Excellent choice, though I don't think you could go wrong with noodles either." Kit grinned at him. "Is that where you went to school? UNC?"

"Undergrad and graduate school. How about you?"

"I got my BS in environmental science from UT-Chattanooga, and my MS in Biology from Georgia Tech."

"No PhD?

"No. Do you have one?"

"No." Alden took another bite of the blueberry bar. He had wanted to pursue a PhD, but the last semester of graduate school had been hard enough. The anxiety attacks were debilitating, and he could barely function on campus. He and Tommy had broken up, and his mother's health had started declining sharply. His therapist had suggested putting off finishing school by another semester, but he'd somehow managed to muddle through. Then he swore never to set foot on a campus again. "So, what do we do if the rain doesn't stop?"

Kit grimaced. "I hate to say it, but we stay put. There's a good chance one direction or the other of the trail will close for flooding. But hey, it's not a huge deal. The folks at the lab know where we are, my car is parked at the trail head. If we're really stuck out here—which, at this point, we're not—they'll send in a search party."

"That sounds serious."

"We're safe and dry where we are." Kit reassured him. "Nothing to worry about."

They ate in silence after that. Alden got the feeling Kit wasn't being completely honest, that he was acting excessively cheery in order to keep Alden's panic at bay. After they finished breakfast, Alden collected the trash and packed it away like he'd seen Kit do yesterday.

Outside, the rain poured down.

SIX

"I don't suppose you brought playing cards?"

Kit glanced up from the paperback he kept in his pack just for moments like this and looked over at Alden, stretched out prone on the floor of the tent and staring back. "Nope."

"Figures." Alden shook his head and scowled. "I'm either three seconds away from panic, or I'm bored out of my mind. I need a distraction. God, how did people live without cell phones? This sucks."

"I could read out loud to you," Kit offered.

"Hmmm, maybe, what is it?" Alden's lips twitched up in one of those sarcastic little smiles of his.

Kit laughed. "*Zen and the Art of Motorcycle Maintenance.*"

"Oh my God, you are such a fucking hippie."

"You like it."

"I kind of do, actually."

Surprised, Kit looked at Alden, whose unguarded grin made him smile back. He put the book down and flopped down next to Alden.

"What can I do to make this easier for you?"

"Unless you have a secret stash of paroxetine, I think I need to just suffer. Sorry I'm being a sasshole."

Alden's hair fell in front of his eyes, and without even thinking, Kit reached out to brush it aside. Alden flinched, then went still, eyes wide.

Tensioned thickened the air between them. This was it. If Kit brushed that hair away from Alden's eyes, he was crossing a line. If he pulled his hand back, he was crossing a different one.

Holding his breath, he pushed the hair back slowly, giving Alden every chance to pull away. When Alden didn't move, Kit kept stroking down the side of his face, running the backs of his fingers along that angular jaw. Blond stubble, too pale to see, scraped his knuckles, then his thumb found the indentation at the center of Alden's chin.

They both froze.

Kit's breath shuddered out from him, and Alden, still staring, parted his lips.

Kit went for it. He caught Alden's upper lip with his lower one. Alden's lips were lush but firm, and as he kissed Kit back, they were wonderfully mobile. Heat lanced through Kit as he pulled Alden closer. Alden gasped and melted into him.

Bodies and mouths, seeking the perfect fit, rolled and pushed. Hands sought skin and tongues sought texture. *Oh god, I'm kissing Alden Kaufman, and it's good—so good.* Kit ran his hands all over Alden's narrow body, wanting to feel everything and unable to get his fill.

Alden didn't seem content to be passively manhandled either—he got a hold of the bottom of Kit's Under Armor and tugged, yanking upward until they had to separate so they could pull it over head and toss it aside.

Their mouths clashed back together, hungry, biting, and all four hands started wrenching Alden's T-shirt up and away.

This time, they paused to take a long look at each other. Kit drank in the sight of Alden's heaving chest, tight pink nipples, and the big bulge in his jeans. He wanted it all.

"Look at you..." Alden sighed, sliding his hands over Kit's chest, stirring up goose bumps and a new surge of lust.

Kit pressed his lips to Alden's throat, tasted the skin there, and felt the way Alden shivered. A moan slipped from him, and the vibration was like a caress on Kit's mouth. He kissed along Alden's shoulders and then down his pecs to latch onto a nipple. His eyes closed with delighted bliss at the sound Alden made when he drew on it, then rubbed it with a thumb.

"Goddamn." The word seemed to rip from Kit's throat in some hoarse voice—his own, yet when had he ever sounded like *that*?

Alden grabbed Kit's hand and moved it down, pressing it to the bulge in those skinny jeans. Kit learned the shape of Alden through the denim, hard, and huge, and he groaned. God, he wanted this. He started stroking, loving all the little noises Alden made as he got more and more turned on.

"Hey, come up here." Alden's voice was quiet, for once not grumpy and cussing, but sort of soft, even tender, and it made Kit's heart ache. Alden drew Kit's mouth back to his and slid his tongue inside. This kiss turned Kit up sweet until he groaned and thrust his cock against Alden's leg.

"Are we really doing this?" If Alden's voice hadn't been so full of wonder, Kit might have been hurt by the way he pulled back and put a hand over his mouth.

"Do you want to stop?" He hoped the answer was no, but he started to pull away just in case.

Alden shook his head and grinned. "No way. Let's get these off, okay?" Alden sat up and unlaced Kit's boots, setting them off to the side. While Alden started on his own boots, Kit shimmied out of his Carhartt's and boxers, then grabbed the hems of Alden's jeans and yanked.

Good god, the man wears tighties.

It wasn't a fetish, exactly, but there were few sights Kit enjoyed more than that of a guy's bulge or ass in a pair of white briefs. All those luscious ridges and curves hinted at under the surface made his mouth water and his body hum with excitement.

He pushed Alden back down to the sleeping bags. "Lie still."

Alden raised one eyebrow, tucked his arm behind his head, and reached for his dick with his other hand. Kit intercepted it, pressed a kiss to the palm, and then nuzzled his face up against that pretty package all wrapped in white cotton. Kit loved that rough, musky smell of man, all concentrated right there. He mouthed Alden through the soft fabric and enjoyed not just Alden's groan but the answering tightening in his own body.

Yeah, they were going to have a good time.

He tongued the notch under the head of Alden's cock, getting the cotton wet and making Alden lurch.

But then Alden grabbed his hair and pulled him back up.

"If you're gonna suck my dick, it's not going to be when I've been sleeping in the woods."

Kit thrilled at the suggestion that they might do this again, somewhere else, someplace where it wasn't just *entertainment* or distraction. But he was getting ahead of himself. First, he had to kiss Alden again. For a long minute, Alden let Kit cover him with his body, taking his weight with a soft sigh as their tongues teased together.

Then they were rolling, and Alden was pushing *Kit* down, leaning over him, and tonguing his nipple. Wet heat spiraled down Kit's spine when a firm hand grabbed his cock and gave it a nice, smooth stroke. The pleasure burst through his body like wildfire.

"Oh, fuck."

He fumbled with Alden's briefs, shoving them down so he

could get a hold of Alden's cock and stroke him in return. Alden's back arched and his dick seemed to strain toward Kit, hard and heavy, a darker shade of pale than the rest of him.

"God, I want to fuck you." Alden's confession ripped out of him and provoked a shudder from Kit. Then he slid his hand down to cup Kit's ass, fingers dipping into the crease. "When I do, I'm gonna eat your ass first, get you all slippery and wet for me, oh, honey, I'll make it so good for you."

"Jesus, Alden." Kit worked his hand faster on Alden's cock. Alden grunted, then started up his dirty talk again, stroking a finger over Kit's tight hole. "I'd be nice, wouldn't make you beg for it—but you would, wouldn't you?"

Kit could feel his orgasm rising in him, but Alden's hand wasn't moving fast enough to get him off. "Come on, man, *please.*"

"Yeah, just like that."

The tip of one of Alden's fingers slid just inside, and then his hand sped up on Kit's dick, and Kit was coming, sobbing out something that sounded like Alden's name.

Alden kissed him then, and it was everything Kit wanted— tender and sweet, and a little desperate and filthy—with both of Alden's hands on him, one on his softening cock and one closing around the hand on his own dick. Kit took the hint, jerking him faster and a little rougher. When Alden tightened up all over, Kit pulled back to watch.

Alden's eyes dropped closed, and he bit down on his lower lip like he was in pain. Then he cried out, and his come splashed all over Kit's belly. Chest heaving, Alden opened his eyes and smiled, not the cocky claim of a conqueror, but the shy entreaty of a supplicant.

"You're fucking intense, you know that?" Kit whispered. "Come here." He pulled Alden in for another kiss, and this time, he took his time, wanting—no, *needing*—Alden to know how *good* he felt, and needing Alden to feel that good too. He ran his hands over Alden's body one last time and smiled into the kiss. "I hope that was a sufficient distraction?"

"That was awesome." Alden laughed. "And it sounds like the rain has stopped."

Kit felt a little twinge of sadness at that, because that meant getting dressed and making their way down the mountain to his car so he could take Alden home to his meds and his data, and they'd have to tell Dr. Evans that they hadn't made the summit, but they sure had mastered teamwork. Except he really didn't think mutual hand jobs was quite going to cut it as an answer when they were asked how they'd learned to work better as a team in the future.

When Alden pulled away, Kit dug a package of unscented wipes out of his pack and handed it over. They cleaned up in a companionable silence, every once in a while laughing at nothing, or pressing a kiss to some exposed bit of skin. Alden-after-sex was sweet and gentle and blushing, and Kit didn't want to take his hands off him.

They were acting like lovers...until the skin was all covered up and they seemed to arrive at some unspoken agreement that the kissing was done.

Alden's hands shook and his brain clicked as he braced himself against a wet tree and tried to catch his breath.

What the fuck had they done? Making out in the tent like they just couldn't get their hands off each other? Hinting that he'd like to do it again? Seeing Kit naked must have short circuited his common sense. That hand job, whispering filthy dirty talk in Kit's ear, would be fantasy fodder for years. But it was stupid. Too much, too intimate. Too appealing.

What the hell had he been thinking?

He'd made up an excuse to get out of the tent and away from Kit, but he couldn't stay out here in the woods all day. He concentrated on calming his heart rate with big, deep breaths. When his hands finally stopped shaking, he went and found Kit breaking down the tent. Hell, he looked so good. The way that brown hair curled over his forehead, and those shoulders of his stretched and bulged under his tight shirt. The way he smiled at Alden, like he saw past the sass to the hot mess inside and still found him sexy.

Goddamn it. Would he ever be able to look at Kit and not think about sex again?

"I don't think we should try for the summit," Kit called as he approached. "I think we should get you home to your medications. The weather could get nastier, so we should take advantage of this break in the rain."

Alden helped Kit pack up the tent, then they shouldered their packs and started down the trail.

"I'm sorry we have to cut the hike short."

Kit shrugged. "S'okay. I'd rather that than you have a panic attack out here, away from your meds or any of your coping mechanisms."

"You found a pretty good way to distract me, back there."

Kit stopped walking and turned around, pointing a finger right in Alden's chest. "I don't have some kind of magic healing dick, Sasshole. The best I can do is get you home."

Alden deflated a little. He'd meant it flirtatiously, but clearly the flirtation was over. Still, Kit didn't have to be a jerk about it.

"I guess your dick's useless to me if it can't heal my agoraphobia. Thanks for the reminder that I was just a pity fuck."

"Is that what you think? God, you're a piece of work." Kit shook his head.

And they'd been getting along so well. "Again, thanks for the reminder."

"We don't have time for your post-coitus friendship sabotage if we're going to get back to my car before dark."

Did that mean Kit thought they were friends? Did Alden want to be friends? He didn't have many friends. Because, yeah, he sabotaged everything. Even Tommy, who had loved him, had accused him of pushing him away at the end.

"I just want to get close to you, and you destroy everything before I have a chance."

They started back down the trail, the creek roaring down below. The sound was almost as soothing as his brown noise. The wet ground was more treacherous than it had been the day before, and a couple of times, Alden slipped in the mud and Kit had to steady him.

"Be careful here." Kit looked over his shoulder and pointed at the ground beneath his feet, and then everything seemed to happen in slow motion. His eyes widened, and he reached for a tree just as his foot slid out from underneath him. He went down, hard, and there was a loud cracking noise.

"Kit!" Alden rushed to his side.

"I'm okay." Kit sat up and pulled a branch out from underneath him. "This snapped, not my leg."

But he wasn't okay. As he tried to stand up and put weight on his leg, he yelped like a kicked puppy.

"What hurts?" Alden asked, offering his shoulder.

"Knee. Holy *shit,* it hurts." Kit wrapped an arm around the offered shoulder, and Alden braced himself against a tree, and together they hauled him upright. Kit's face contorted in pain and his breath was coming hard.

"Let's get your pack off your shoulders." Alden reached for it, keeping one hand braced on the tree so he wouldn't fall.

"Give me a minute—I'll be okay in just a minute."

But he wasn't okay. Every time he tried to put weight on his leg, he would hiss in pain and grab the tree again.

"Kit, honey, we need to get you sitting down. This isn't something you can fuck around with."

"I need to get you off the goddamn trail so you can get to your meds!" Kit growled in frustration.

"Hey. Look at me." Alden grabbed Kit's face between both hands and pressed their foreheads together. "I can do this. Not having my meds sucks, yes, and my brain is flicking like crazy, yes. I could have a panic attack out here and have to suffer through it, yes. I'm not going to deny that all of those things are fucking awful. But you are *not* responsible for getting me to my meds. You can't walk, let alone hike, so sit your pretty ass down and let's brainstorm like goddamn scientists."

Kit knocked Alden's hands away, and then he laughed and dug the heels of his hands into his eyes. Finally, he looked at Alden. "Are you telling me you don't need a hero?"

Alden shuddered. He hated that word. "Never."

"Okay, then you can be *my* hero." Kit let Alden slip his pack off his shoulders and set it aside. "We passed a campsite about a quarter mile back. Can you carry both packs?"

Alden looked him over. Surely he wasn't going to try to hike that quarter mile? "And what would you be doing?"

"I'm going to try to fol—"

"Oh no. I'll get our packs back there and set up the tent, then I'm coming back for you. Sit down." Alden gestured to a fallen tree on the side of the trail. "That looks like it can hold a mountain man."

With help, Kit was able to get to the side of the trail, and he even sat without complaining.

"Good man," Alden said. He picked up Kit's pack—which was lighter than his own even though he was *sure* there was more stuff in it—slung it awkwardly over his shoulder, and started up the trail.

"Alden—"

He turned back. "Yeah?"

"I liked it when you called me 'honey'." Kit's pained smile was half-apology.

Alden's heart thundered in his chest. He didn't even realize he'd done that. *Endearments, really?* But for the life of him, he couldn't come up with a snide comeback, so he told the truth instead.

"Me too."

It took longer than it should have to get to the campsite, thanks to the slippery mud. He was thankful, once he arrived, that he had paid attention while they pitched the tent the night before. He set it up carefully on the tent pad, then shoved their packs inside and zipped it closed.

Brain click.

Now he just had to get Kit back here and figure out how to get him off the mountain.

Kit was restless and jumpy waiting for Alden to return. His knee felt okay—ish—as long as he didn't put any weight on it, but then when he did, a sharp pain would flare up along the side of his leg. *Dammit.* This was a disaster.

And what the hell was he going to do about Alden? They'd crossed a line by having sex, and neither of them seemed to have any idea what to do next. They couldn't pretend it hadn't happened and go back to snarking at each other like insecure assholes. For one thing, Kit wasn't any good at pretending. For another, the snark *hurt* now. And he didn't want to hurt Alden.

He wasn't any closer to understanding him, but he liked him a lot more than he had the day before.

He hadn't given much thought to how Alden had become agoraphobic, but now he wished he'd asked. And how was Alden coping with being out there in the woods by himself?

Kit tried to stand up again, and without the pack, he found it easier to shuffle a few feet up the trail. His left knee still hurt like hell, and it wouldn't bear his weight, but if he wrapped his hand around a tree and hopped—

Of course that's when Alden came around the bend up ahead. He scowled the moment he saw Kit.

"What the hell are you doing?" Rushing to Kit's side, Alden ducked under his shoulder and wrapped an arm around his waist. "You should have waited for me."

"I was just testing it out." Blood rushed to Kit's face. "I'm embarrassed."

"Embarrassed you got hurt?" Alden looked up at him. "Or embarrassed you got caught trying to walk on it like a fucking idiot?"

Kit laughed and let himself lean on Alden. Even though Alden was smaller than he was, he was fit and strong, and he took Kit's weight without flinching. "Both."

"Come on, let's get you to the campsite, and we'll make an action plan. I set up the tent so you can have a dry place to sit. I think we should try calling 9-1-1, even though we don't have signal—I'm pretty sure they send someone out for an incomplete call."

Kit was impressed. "Yeah, that's basically Hiking 101. I should have thought of it mys—ah!" He winced as pain shot up his leg when he put too much weight down. Alden simply held onto him, waiting for him to catch his breath. Kit appreciated that steadying touch and the comfort it offered. "—Myself," he finished.

"You had other things on your mind." Alden's voice was muffled against Kit's chest, his breath warm through Kit's shirt. Kit couldn't help himself; he gave Alden a gentle, one-armed squeeze, just barely, even though he doubted his prickly hiking partner would be receptive to that tiny expression of affection.

Alden went still and silent, and then gave Kit an even tinier squeeze back.

It wasn't much, but it was *something.*

Following Alden's terse instructions to "just fucking let me take your weight," Kit managed to hobble to the campsite without hurting himself further. He held onto a tree for balance as Alden unzipped the tent and gestured inside.

"Do you need help getting in there?"

Kit shook his head. "I don't think so."

But maneuvering himself down low enough to scoot inside was troublesome, and Alden helped him anyway. "It's not weak to ask for help."

"I know."

"I'm going to call 9-1-1 now, okay?"

Kit nodded. "Thank you."

Alden paced around the campsite with his phone to his ear, but returned to the tent without saying anything.

"No signal. I hope it was enough. I wish we had a sat phone. How are you?"

"I'd be better if you'd wait in here with me." Kit patted the ground next to himself, and Alden crawled into the tent.

They stared at each other for a long moment, then both started talking at once.

"Do you want to—"

"We should talk about—"

Kit laughed. "Go ahead."

"I liked fooling around with you this morning," Alden said. "But I don't want to give you the impression that I am into—" He broke off. Then ran a hand through his hair, ruffling it. "I like you. I like being friends with you. But I'm not relationship material. I didn't want you to have the wrong impression."

Kit sighed. Of course Alden had been worrying about this too. "Alden, it was just two friends passing the time. I'm not expecting anything from you, okay?"

Alden nodded. "Okay. Good. And I'm sorry."

"What are you sorry for?" Kit watched as Alden's eyebrows drew together and he scowled.

"For calling it a pity fuck? For putting words in your mouth. For being an asshole." He shrugged. "Take your pick."

"I accept your apology. And I'm sorry for being bossy and short-tempered."

"Well, I accept your apology, too." Alden smiled. "Now come here."

Alden helped Kit maneuver around so he was sitting between Alden's legs, his back to Alden's chest, foot propped up on the pack, and Alden's arms around his waist. Alden rested his cheek against Kit's back.

"Better?"

Kit relaxed into the embrace. "This is nice. I'm not used to someone fussing over me." And he certainly didn't expect Alden to be comforting him.

"Well, don't get too used to it. I'm just taking advantage of your body heat. You're like a very muscular space heater."

Kit laughed. "Happy to help."

It started to rain again, and Kit zipped the tent flap closed to keep it outside. Their situation looked worse by the minute, and he couldn't help but send out a fervent prayer. *Please don't let the trail flood. Please.*

SEVEN

Alden tried again to call 9-1-1 and also to send text messages to their colleagues to ask them for help, but the messages didn't go through. He focused on keeping Kit comfortable to hold the panic at bay, and for the most part, it worked.

It was hours before help arrived, but when it did, the EMTs moved quickly and efficiently to stabilize Kit's knee and move him onto a stretcher to carry him down the mountain while Alden broke down the tent.

"How did you know where to find us?"

"Your friends called 9-1-1 when you didn't reach the summit and they couldn't reach you by phone or text."

"Is the trail flooded?" he asked.

"No, but the ground is soft," one of the EMTs answered as they hefted the stretcher.

Alden followed, struggling to carry both packs.

When they arrived at the trail head, Alden watched helplessly as they bundled Kit into an ambulance. He hated ambulances. And hospitals. And his guts wrenched at the sight of Kit being hauled off to one.

"I'll be fine." Kit smiled at him. "Just don't wreck my car, okay?"

And then he was gone. Alden typed the hospital address into his phone and whispered a quick prayer to any God who would listen that he could hold it together once he got there. He hadn't set foot inside a hospital since the last time he'd been treated in one...and he refused to let his mind go there. His mother's assisted living community—which, in certain areas looked just enough like a doctor's office to freak him out—was stressful enough.

The rain resumed and traffic slowed to a crawl on the road winding down out of the mountains toward Asheville. Dammit, why did Kit have to get hurt? He could be safely on his way home by now, maybe even sitting in comfort on his own couch with a cold beer and his feet up in perfectly normal stupid cotton socks.

His brain clicked, and he told Siri to play his brown noise. When he finally reached the hospital, the sound had soothed him enough that he was no longer on the verge of a panic attack. He parked Kit's Explorer and sat for a long moment. He could get an Uber back to his car. But he needed to return Kit's keys. It's not like he could just hand them to a random stranger and say, *"Give these to the giant with a limp."*

He had to go inside.

Taking a deep breath, he started focusing inward, relaxing his muscles and pushing the panic away. Therapy had given him the tools for this. He could do this. People in hospitals were there to help.

He turned off the car and climbed out, locking it behind him and making his way to the emergency room door. He stopped at the desk where a tall, slender woman was entering information into a computer. He could do this. He could talk to a stranger. He could pretend they were anywhere else other than a hospital. Except that was absurd. *Just fucking talk, Alden.*

"Can I help you?" She looked up at him over the rims of reading glasses.

"Hi. I was with my friend and he got hurt. The ambulance brought him here, and I followed with his car. Can you get his keys to him?" The words tumbled out of his mouth in a rush.

"Name?" she looked up expectantly.

"Ald—sorry. You mean his name. Kit Taylor."

"You can give them to him yourself if you like." She pointed at a double door. "He's in a waiting room right through there."

"Thank you." He pushed through the door, and sure enough, there was Kit, one foot propped on a chair. Even injured, Kit looked powerful, a perfect image of masculine beauty and strength. Lucky bastard.

"Hey," Alden said, and Kit looked up, his face tired.

"Hey. You made it."

Alden nodded shakily and eased himself into the chair next to Kit's, trying not to look around, trying even harder to tune out the smells and the sounds and the bland industrial decor. "Traffic was a bitch. Been waiting long?"

Kit shook his head. "Not too bad."

"I brought your keys." Alden handed them over. "So, I should—"

"Why don't you—" Kit laughed. "You go first."

"I should go. I have to take an Uber back to my car."

"Stay, and I'll drive you over once I'm done here."

Alden winced. "I really hate hospitals." Understatement of the century.

"Please? I'll buy you dinner. I don't want to be alone."

Oh, for fuck's sake. Alden's irritation almost provoked him to snap at Kit, but he looked up instead, and met Kit's open gaze. He looked uncomfortable and vulnerable, and even though

Alden wanted to run like hell, he couldn't leave Kit like this. They were a team, after all.

"Okay."

A sunny smile broke out on Kit's face. "Thank you."

"Mr. Taylor?" A nurse stepped into the waiting room with a wheelchair. "Come on back, we've got a room ready for you." He wheeled the chair up right next to Kit's and then smoothly helped Kit transfer into the chair.

Alden watched, his head growing light as the scene triggered a memory of gentle, competent hands helping him shift himself into a chair, pain lancing through his body. The smells, the sounds—everything pushed in on him.

"I have to go," he blurted out, standing and walking blindly toward the doors. "I have to—" Nausea swept over him just as he reached them.

And then he fell.

Kit watched in horror as Alden fell face first into the doors and the nurse rushed to his side.

"Sir! Sir—"

Another nurse rushed from an open room and helped him roll Alden over. Alden's face looked ashy green, like he was about to throw up, but he sat up with the help of the two nurses, and then he pushed them both away.

"I can't be here, I can't, I have to go. I have to *go*." Alden tried to stand.

"Whoa, whoa. Slow down." The male nurse glanced at the woman who had run out to help him. "He's not even a patient, he just fainted."

"You can't keep me here. You can't make me stay here. Kit, tell them I'm okay."

Kit glanced helplessly at the nurses. "He needs to get home; he hasn't had his medication today."

Apparently, that was the wrong thing to say. Alden shot him a furious glare, and the nurses both sprang into action. Before Kit knew it, he was being wheeled away while the lady nurse wrapped a blood pressure cuff around Alden's arm.

"He's going to be okay; he just needs his anxiety meds." Kit told the nurse.

"We'll take care of him, don't worry. Let's get you down to imaging and find out what you did to your knee."

The X-ray was quick, but the MRI felt like an eternity. Lying still as could be in that cold, loud room while the headphones blared old pop standbys, he had nothing to do but worry about Alden. The ashen color of his face as he fell, the haunted expression the moment before—and then the fury when Kit said he needed his meds. The betrayal on his face had made it absolutely clear: Alden would never forgive him.

And they'd just started to become friends. Ish. Two guys who got along well enough and exchanged a mutual hand job. That was friendly. And he'd agreed to let Kit buy him dinner—well, he'd been coerced and guilt tripped into letting Kit buy him dinner. And then this.

The MRI machine fell silent.

"You're all done." The tech pulled him clear of the machine and helped him into the wheelchair. She was a short Black woman with purple hair plaited in with her own in braids that hung all the way down her back. "Great job holding so still. I'm going to put you in a room, and the doc's gonna look at this and let you know what's up, okay?"

"Thank you."

It was an eternity later when the doctor finally came in.

"Well, Mr. Taylor, you're not going to be hiking for a while. I'm sorry." She frowned down at his chart. "You've torn the anterior cruciate ligament on your left knee—your ACL. Thankfully, you're young and fit, so after surgery and some rehab, you should be fine. I'm going to refer you to an orthopedic specialist to perform the surgery. You'll want to schedule that appointment as soon as possible. In the meantime, stay off it, keep ice on it, and don't overdo it. There will be a prescription with your discharge paperwork to help you manage the pain."

"Do you know where my friend is? He fainted in the waiting room. Is he still here?"

She looked up at him. "I'll ask your nurse to find out."

He nodded. "Thank you."

"You can get dressed—Kevin will be in shortly to go over your prescription dosage and discharge instructions. Unless you have any questions for me?"

He shook his head, thoughts turning immediately to Alden.

Alden found Kit in a room not far from his own.

"You're still here?" Kit looked up at Alden, surprise etched across his face. "When the nurse said they'd discharged you, I'd have thought you'd have gone home." His leg was braced, and a pair of crutches stood in the corner, but he was pulling his boots back on.

"They only just discharged me about ten minutes ago, and then I had to figure out which room you were in. I don't like hospitals. They wanted to do a psych eval." Alden didn't know whether he found that a relief or just fucking annoying. Luckily, he'd gotten his regular therapist on the phone, and she'd explained his situation. *Post-traumatic stress disorder and agoraphobia.* And *then* they'd offered him Xanax.

"Because you fainted in the waiting room? Or because I fucked up and told them you just needed your meds?" Kit gestured him closer, and Alden went. "Thanks, by the way, for waiting with me. I'm sorry. I'm so sorry I didn't take better care of everything."

"Don't apologize to me, you're the one on crutches. And it's fine." It might have been the Xanax talking, but he really did feel fine. A little sleepy maybe, but he was used to that when he was on benzos.

In the bright light of the hospital room, Kit looked tired and drawn and surprisingly small until he smiled at Alden. The sheer magnitude of his presence seemed to depend on that smile. "I'm glad you're fine. I'm not fine. Torn ACL. Apparently, I need surgery. The Costa Rica job is definitely not going to be in my future."

A wave of disappointment for Kit washed over Alden. He knew what it was like to have to give up an opportunity through no choice of his own. "I'm sorry, I know how much that meant to you."

"There will be other jobs. I'm disappointed, though."

Alden nodded. "Of course you are. I would be too."

"I'm going to have to call Dr. Evans and figure out whether I need to take short term disability or what. The logistics of this are overwhelming. And my apartment is on the second floor. This could get—well—" Kit waved at the crutches. "—Interesting."

"I have some experience with this stuff." Alden said slowly. "From when my mom was still living with me. My house—" What was he doing? He wasn't going to offer to let the mountain man recuperate at his place, was he? But he was somewhat responsible for Kit falling down the mountain in the first place. "My house is totally handicap accessible—for my mom, but, um, since she doesn't live with me anymore, there's an extra room."

Kit's eyebrows drew together, and he frowned at Alden. "Are you—but you don't even like me."

Face flushing hot, Alden looked down at his shoes. "You're all right."

"I'm all right?" Kit smirked back at him. "Just all right?"

"You're as enthusiastic as a puppy and only half as charming. But you give a good hand job and your taste in music doesn't suck. You wanna stay with me or not?"

Kit threw his head back and laughed. "That's the sasshole I know. If you're sure I won't be in your way."

Alden shrugged. "I'm sure you will be. But we'll cross that bridge when we get to it. Can you drive?"

Kit looked at his knee. "They shot my knee full of local anesthesia. I don't feel a thing right now. And I have an automatic transmission, but my discharge paperwork said not to drive."

"Damn." Alden should have known. "They gave me Xanax, and I'll be too dopey to drive for a bit. Well, we can get a cab, take it to your place and get what you need. I can take an Uber to collect the cars in the morning."

EIGHT

Kit lived in a quiet suburban apartment complex not far from Alden's house. When the cab pulled up to his building, he reached for his crutches and started to get out of the car. Alden stopped him with a hand on his arm.

"I can move a lot faster than you can right now. Do you trust me to get what you need for you?"

Kit nodded. "My toothpaste and toothbrush are already in my camping pack. I just need clothes and my laptop."

"Do you have roommates? How do I find your bedroom?"

"No roommates. And it's the only one."

"Favorite coffee mug, weighted blanket, anything like that?"

Kit's smile grew more bemused. "A coffee mug is a coffee mug. I'm not attached. But in the cupboard above the coffee pot, there's some herbal tea and an electric kettle."

"I'll get them." Alden held out his hand for the keys. "I assume you don't have pets? Since you're in the field so much and you don't have roommates? Any houseplants need watering?"

Kit shook his head and dropped the keys into Alden's palm. "No pets and no plants."

"Be right back."

Kit's apartment was scrupulously clean, only one mug upside down in the drying rack next to the sink. The tea and kettle were easy to find, so he set them on the counter next to the charging laptop and moved on. Kit's bedroom offered no hints to his personality. Bare walls, a simple blue comforter on the bed. It was spare and quiet. A few photos on the dresser showed Kit with people Alden assumed must be his family. An older couple —Kit clearly got his height and his megawatt smile from his dad and the brown curls from his mom—and then one of him with two little girls, one of whom held a frog out toward the camera, grinning wildly. The nieces were seriously cute.

He opened the top drawer of the dresser to find a neatly folded row of boxer shorts and a bundle of socks in tidy pairs. He pulled out seven of each, then made his way down the dresser. Five short sleeved T-shirts. Three pairs of jeans. Three more of sweatpants. Two of those cargo pants Kit wore camping.

He looked around for something to carry them in, finding an empty laundry basket at the foot of the bed. He dumped the armload of clothes into it, then made his way to the closet. A row of neat henleys in dark, masculine shades. Alden picked out a few of them—blue and green and gray. A soft, cream-colored sweater that felt like cashmere. Two of the plaid flannels.

His phone buzzed with a text.

Grab my robe?

He smiled and checked the back of the bathroom door. There it was.

Got it.

With his laundry basket loaded down, he picked up a pair of running shoes from the floor of the closet, put the laptop and the tea supplies on top of the clothes, turned off all the lights, and let himself out.

He put Kit's belongings in the trunk of the cab with their camping packs and climbed into the back seat, handing Kit the keys.

"If I got it all wrong, you can blame the Xanax."

"I'm sure it's fine." Kit smiled. "Are you sure you still want me to stay with you?"

Alden smiled back. "Sure. It'll be nice to have someone else in the house. A little weird, maybe, but nice."

"Thank you."

Alden gave his address to the cab driver, and before he knew it, he was handing over his debit card to pay, and he and Kit were left standing on the sidewalk in front of his house.

"We're here."

———

Kit followed as Alden opened the door to the kitchen and ushered him inside. "The living room is right through there. Park yourself on the couch and I'll bring our stuff in." Before Kit could say anything, Alden bustled back outside, clearly taking charge. Okay then.

He crutched his way past the kitchen table in the direction Alden had pointed, switching on the lights as he went. Alden's house was not at all what he expected. The kitchen was warm and cozy with persimmon-colored walls and travertine counter-tops. The living room was dominated by a big purple sofa and an antique trunk serving as a coffee table. Art deco style travel posters decorated the walls, and a fish tank stood in one corner, lights dimmed for the evening. Kit set his crutches to the side and sank into the sofa. Heavenly.

The sounds of Alden moving around made him fidgety. He didn't like having someone else taking care of him. Especially not the prickly coworker he was quickly learning was not as prickly as he'd thought.

"Hey, Alden?" He called out. A moment later Alden appeared in the doorway.

"Hmm?"

"What do you like on your pizza? I promised you dinner—at the very least I can order in."

"And here I was planning to devour your stash of energy bars." Alden said archly. "Any meat is fine, and mushrooms are cool, but I absolutely hate green peppers."

"Pineapple?" Kit raised a brow.

"I am not nearly high enough for that." Alden cringed. "Sorry if that's your thing."

Kit laughed, trying to picture Alden with the munchies. "I actually just like the basics. Cheese, pepperoni. Mushrooms are, as you said, cool."

"That sounds good to me. Maybe black olives too?" Alden suggested. "I like my pizza salty."

"Like I like my men," Kit answered. "Do you have a favorite place to order from?"

Alden smiled. "Wherever is fine. Thank you for thinking of it."

"You're welcome." Kit pulled out his phone, pulled up the delivery app, and placed the order.

Alden brought his laptop to him on the couch. "You can plug it in wherever you like. There's a power strip next to the side table that's probably the most convenient."

"Thank you."

"I'm going to hang your clothes in the guest room closet. Do you want dibs on the first shower? I have two bathrooms, but I don't think my old-ass water heater can handle simultaneous showers."

Kit shook his head. "You go ahead."

He listened as Alden moved through the hallway, turning on lights and humming to himself. Humming. He really was a different man in the comfort of his own home. Or maybe it was the drugs they'd given him at the hospital. Down the hall, a shower turned on, and Kit pictured Alden stripping off his camping clothes and standing under the spray.

The thought got him hard. Had it only been that morning that the two of them had jerked each other off in the tent? Kissing and touching, dirty talk and roaming hands. How did that even happen? *Boredom. Alden was bored. He doesn't want you like that.*

Kit would have to be careful not to take advantage of Alden's hospitality to seek a second round, but the idea of it still held a lot of appeal. Especially when he remembered Alden's whispers about fucking him. That was fantasy fodder from a heated moment, not a promise. Not even a hint.

The water turned off. A few minutes later, Alden appeared, his blond hair dark and wet, combed back from his face. He wore plaid pajama pants and a gray tank top. "Shower's all yours. I'll show you your room now?"

Kit nodded and used the crutches and the coffee table to help heft himself off the couch. "This is going to take some getting used to."

"I know, but it will get easier. And then after your surgery, you'll be back on your feet, hiking through the woods in no time. This is you."

Alden pushed open a door. Kit's laundry basket, now empty, sat beside a queen-size bed. A walk-in closet held all his clothes, and a double door opened into a huge ensuite bath. It was clearly a master suite, not a guest room.

"This isn't your room?" Kit asked.

"No, this was mom's room. I use one of the other bedrooms

as my office. The last one has been my bedroom since high school. It didn't feel right moving into this room."

"Right." Kit could see that.

"Let me get you some shampoo and soap." Alden disappeared down the hallway again, reappearing with a full bottle of shampoo and a bar of soap still in the box. "I'll put these in the shower. Your backpack is next to the bed. I didn't know if you cared whether I unpacked it or not, so I left it."

"Thank you."

"I'll leave you to it." Alden disappeared into the en suite bath, and then reappeared, smiled tightly, and left, shutting the door behind him.

Kit sat on the bed and eased his hiking boots off. The numbness in his knee was starting to wear off. He glanced around, and sure enough, Alden had left his prescription by the bed, along with a glass of water. Kit took one of the painkillers, washing it down with about half the glass. Then he finished removing his clothes and tossed them into the laundry basket.

Getting himself into the bathroom on crutches was easier than he thought it would be. The doorway was wide, and there was plenty of room to maneuver. The shower was large and tiled from floor to ceiling. A long teak bench stretched along one side. Alden had unwrapped the soap and left it on a wooden dish on the bench, with the shampoo next to it. A towel and washcloth were at the far end of the bench, away from the reach of the water, but where Kit wouldn't have to stand to reach them. So thoughtful. Kit turned on the water, carefully balanced his crutches against the wall, and eased himself into the spray. The soap wasn't the no-frills supermarket soap he was used to, but something silky feeling that smelled like sage and citrus and just a little bit like patchouli. It smelled like Alden, he realized as he lathered it over his chest and arms, down his stomach to his groin.

If anyone had told him when he woke up yesterday morning that he'd finish the weekend in Alden Kaufman's house, preparing to sleep there for the next few weeks, he'd have laughed in their face. And yet now, with the memory of Alden's hands and the smell of his soap on his skin, he was fiercely glad. Whatever came next, he didn't have to face it alone.

NINE

"November third? That's three weeks away." Kit's voice echoed down the hallway to where Alden tried very hard not to eavesdrop. "No. No, I understand. Of course. Can I be put on a list in case something comes available sooner? Yes. Okay, thank you. Yeah, it's Christopher Taylor. Date of birth..."

Christopher. Alden knew that Kit was a nickname, but he had a hard time reconciling the idea of his mountain man having a name so...ordinary.

His mountain man. What on earth was he doing thinking like that? He'd let a hand job go to his head, and now he had an injured roommate he couldn't stop mooning over. Kit Taylor was a bad idea.

But that bad idea had made coffee and had bagels delivered this morning right before calling Dr. Evans and explaining that he was out of commission for fieldwork until after he'd recovered from surgery. Alden had eavesdropped on that conversation too. Kit had just casually mentioned that he was staying with Alden for the time being, like the injury wasn't a complete upheaval in his life or Alden's. Just good buddies helping each other out.

Alden resolutely looked back at his computer screen, where Excel spreadsheets made sense, because it was far easier than trying to figure out how complicated his work life was about to get.

A few minutes later, Kit appeared in his office doorway. He set his crutches deep under his arms, crossed his arms over his chest and leaned, filling the frame. Alden tried not to notice the way Kit's henley stretched and molded itself across his muscles, staring instead at the spreadsheet in front of him.

"Hey. It's going to be awhile before I can get a surgery date with the orthopedic specialist. They've got me for a pre-op consult on November third."

Alden looked up. "Sounds like you'll be here for a while. Would you like me to go pick up more of your stuff?"

Kit dropped his arms and then ran one of his hands through his tousled curls. "Maybe. Are you sure you're okay with this?

Alden bit back a laugh. Of course he wasn't sure. But he'd made his bed. "It's fine. I don't mind your company. And the bagels this morning were really good."

"I appreciate your hospitality. The least I can do is feed you."

"I have—" Alden gestured to his screen. "—a bunch of reports to look at today. I'm sorry, why don't we talk later?"

Kit immediately looked apologetic. "Later—right. I'm sorry. I'll just—" He looked around. "Read in the living room maybe? Or will I be in your way there?"

Oh, for fuck's sake. "You aren't in my way, Kit. But I'm working. I know a lot of people think working from home means you can fuck off as much as you work, but that's not what it's like for me. When I'm in this room, I'm working, and I need to focus. Everywhere else, I'm fair game, okay?"

"I'm sorry."

"Stop apologizing and GTFO."

"Right."

Kit disappeared from his doorway, and Alden reached for his noise-cancelling headphones. This was going to take some getting used to.

An hour later, when he broke for lunch, he found Kit sprawled on the couch, nose buried in a book.

"Hey," he called out on his way to the kitchen. "I'm going to make a sandwich, you want anything? I can make you one too, or heat up some leftover pizza?"

Kit glanced up from the book. "What kind of sandwich?"

"Pastrami on rye. I also have turkey. Swiss cheese or American."

"What you're having sounds amazing. This book, by the way, is fucking awesome."

Alden glanced at the cover. Ah, yes. A gay urban fantasy with psychic cops. It was pretty fucking awesome. "Yeah, that author is one of my favorites."

Kit reached for his crutches, but Alden stopped him. "No, stay put. I'll bring the sandwiches out here. Did you get to the part where they find the first body yet?"

"No—don't tell me anything." Kit picked up the book again. "I want to be surprised."

Alden piled the pastrami high on two sandwiches, calling out "Mustard?" and proceeding when Kit answered in the affirmative. He cut them on the diagonal, added a pickle spear to each plate, and grabbed a bag of potato chips from the pantry.

"Here." He handed Kit a plate and sat at the other end of the couch, legs crossed and his plate in his lap. He set the bag of chips on the couch between them. "Hope you like salt and vinegar."

"My favorite." Kit grinned. "Thank you."

"So, that book series is at least ten books long. I don't know that it will get you through three weeks, but..."

Kit laughed. "I *am* going back to work. Not field work, obviously. But Dr. Evans said there's plenty of administrative stuff I can help out with, or I can be your bitch for the next month or so."

Alden nodded. He didn't really work well with others, but since Kit was here, no reason not to get his insight on some of the projects they were working on, so he said as much.

"You work fine with others," Kit disagreed. "As long as you don't have to see them face to face."

Alden shrugged. That wasn't exactly true, but how was Kit supposed to understand the nuances of Alden's agoraphobia when he didn't understand it completely himself?

"You're different, here." Kit gestured around the room. "In your house, you're so much more personable. Not as uptight."

"I'm only an asshole in public?" Alden arched a brow and took another bite of his sandwich.

"Not exactly. Maybe." Kit studied him, and Alden stare back, fighting the urge to look away. "No—it's not that. It's that you aren't looking for a fight here."

"I'm not looking for a fight out there either." Alden shook his head. "Don't try to make sense of me. Let's psychoanalyze you instead. Why is your apartment so sterile?"

Kit laughed. "Real answer? Because I don't really live there. It's just a place to sleep."

"So where's home?"

Kit pondered that in silence, chewing slowly. Finally he answered, "I used to think Tennessee was still home, but that's not true anymore. Maybe the great outdoors. Maybe my tent. Maybe, as soft and comfortable as it is, this outrageously purple velvet couch of yours."

It was outrageous, and that's why Alden loved it. "Maybe if you had an outrageously purple couch, you'd feel like your place was home too."

"Maybe I would. I have a hard time reconciling you with all

this color. The orange kitchen, the purple couch. The iridescent glass tile in the bathroom. Who are you?"

"I'm a guy who likes color. And this is my home."

"And the travel posters? Places you'd like to visit or places you have?"

Alden took another bite of his sandwich rather than describe the family trips around the country when he was a kid, visiting various national parks. If he started talking about his childhood, he would have to talk about his family, and he just couldn't do it. Not with Kit, not with anybody.

Kit seemed to pick up on his reticence. "Sorry. That was nosy. So, you like color. What's your favorite?"

"Deep teal, like the ocean seen from above," he answered without hesitation. "You?"

"Green, like the forest. Did you decorate this place? Or did your mom?"

Alden laughed. His mom's taste in decor trended much more toward Raggedy Ann dolls and wooden furniture with hearts and flowers painted on it. "I did, after she moved out. With her blessing."

"Are you going to see her this weekend?"

"Yes. Why, do you want to come with me?" Alden tossed it out like a joke, but Kit seemed to actually ponder the question.

"I'm really curious about your mom, but—I think I would be intruding."

"Maybe next time." Alden polished off the last of his sandwich and picked up his pickle spear and pointed it at Kit. "I definitely have to tell her there's someone staying here with me though. She's going to want to know everything about you."

Kit laughed, a big rumble that shook the couch. "Is there a questionnaire or something I should fill out, or do I just have to count on you to get it right?"

"Don't worry, I won't be telling her about the hand jobs. I'll just leave it at 'tall, handsome, good manners.' I don't suppose you're secretly very wealthy? Maybe a Greek tycoon? She would love that."

The couch shook again as Kit hooted with laughter. "I wish. Unfortunately, I work for the United States government. Good benefits, though."

"Never underestimate the appeal of a steady job."

"Speaking of." Kit glanced at his laptop. "I'm going to need somewhere I can work—is it okay if I take your kitchen table hostage?"

"That's fine. I don't actually sit at it often. Not unless I've got company."

"That happen a lot?"

Alden shook his head. He wasn't about to tell Kit about Tommy's occasional booty calls. Those happened maybe once a year at most, and explaining Tommy to Kit was another of those things he didn't have words for. They might be starting to be friends, but they weren't about to bare their souls or anything. "I mean, you're here. But no, not usually."

"Thank you, then. I'll set up at the table. I think Dr. Evans is going to put me in charge of the team newsletter or something like that."

"We have a team newsletter?" Alden was baffled by that. He didn't get a team newsletter.

"It was a joke. We don't really. Just those notes from Stella when someone has a birthday so we can all stop by and sign the card."

Alden never signed the cards. The combination of guilt and longing that filled him at the idea of missing out on something so normal surprised him. Usually, he could tamp down those feelings. Usually.

"Well, I have to get back to work." Alden reached for Kit's plate. "I'll take that."

"I can wash the dishes. After all, you made the sandwiches. Which were delicious by the way."

"You will break my plates trying to carry them on your crutches. No thank you. Just stay put and read your book."

Kit looked like he was going to protest again, but Alden silenced him with what he hoped was a stern glare.

The last thing he needed was Kit hurting himself worse trying to be helpful.

Kit and Alden quickly fell into a comfortable routine. Kit, always an early riser, made coffee for two in the mornings, which they shared at the table in companionable silence, checking their phones and scrolling through the day's headlines and social media feeds. Sometimes, Alden would hand his phone across the table to share something amusing with Kit, and Kit found himself doing the same as he grew more accustomed to Alden's sly sense of wit. Eventually Alden would stand, stretch, and offer Kit a parting smile before holing up in his office with his reports.

Kit wasn't used to the type of work Alden had him doing—organizing reports and spreadsheets and calling into conference calls to take notes—but he was glad to have the work because it meant he wasn't going stir-crazy on Alden's giant couch. Some days, Alden didn't come out of his office until long after the lunch hour had passed, but others he'd come stalking into the kitchen with a scowl and start digging through the fridge, only to startle when he turned and saw Kit at the table.

"Did you forget I was here?" Kit tried not to laugh. It was Friday, and he'd been there almost two weeks, and Alden was still jumpy.

Alden scowled, then brushed it off with a flutter of his hand.

"No. You're just so much bigger than normal people, it's always a surprise."

Kit bit back a flirtatious reply—that hand job in the woods seemed like a lifetime ago, and Alden had given no hints he'd be into a repeat performance. A joke about his size was *not* going to defuse whatever was going on.

"Are you sure that's it? I don't want to add to your anxiety. Is my being here making you feel unsafe?"

Alden stilled and cocked his head to one side. "Why would you say that?"

Kit shrugged, casting about for the right words. "You just seem so jumpy when you see me, like one of those videos of a cat that gets surprised by a cucumber. I know you said your agoraphobia is tied to feeling safe. I'm in your house, and I seem more comfortable here than you do."

Sighing, Alden dropped the food in his hands onto the counter. "That was my dad's chair. I'm not used to seeing anyone sitting there. It's stupid."

"Oh." Kit looked down at the table, heat flushing through him. He'd never thought to ask about things like that. "Should I sit somewhere else?"

Alden shook his head. "No. Please don't. You're my guest, you should sit wherever you're most comfortable." A horrified look crossed his face. "Unless I've just made you uncomfortable by telling you that. It's not haunted or anything."

"Of course not. Come here." Kit would have preferred to stand and cross the room himself, but the crutches and the knee brace made it difficult. Alden sat across the table from Kit and crossed his arms over his chest, his facial expression stoic and closed off.

Kit scrubbed a hand over his face to keep from reaching for Alden with it. "Do you want to talk about it?"

Alden's eyes widened. "Absolutely not." He stood and

returned to fixing his lunch, then took his sandwich back to the office and closed the door without another word.

Kit didn't know what to say or do. He hadn't expected Alden to want to talk—the guy clammed up tight anytime Kit tried to find out anything about his family—but the abrupt shutdown followed by silence? Well, he hadn't expected that either. Late in the afternoon, when he hadn't seen so much as Alden's empty plate return to the kitchen, he decided to do something about the awkwardness.

Alden had done most of the cooking since Kit had moved in, brushing off Kit's offers to help with a firm, *"I'm used to my routines."*

But Kit knew as often as Alden skipped lunch, he was prone to working through dinner too, coming out of his cave only when hunger finally drove him out.

Kit found what he needed for a hearty chicken soup and went to work peeling vegetables and browning them in the pot before adding chicken and broth. He tossed the ends and peels into the compost bin, pleased with himself. Once the chicken was cooked through, he added rice and adjusted the seasonings. Once everything was ready, he crutched his way down the hall to Alden's office door and knocked.

"What is it?" Alden opened the door and peered up at Kit through his reading glasses, looking wary.

"Dinner time." Kit grinned.

Alden took a step back and glanced over his shoulder. "I still—"

"It can wait. You need to eat. Come on, I made soup."

"What kind of soup?" Alden's voice lilted up at the end of the question.

"Chicken and rice. And not out of a can."

"You made me chicken soup with rice? From scratch? After the way I treated you this afternoon?" The surprise in Alden's voice broke Kit's heart. Alden really wasn't used to anyone doing nice things for him.

"Comfort food. You seemed like you could use a little comfort. Come on." Kit grabbed Alden's hand and gave it a squeeze. "Let's eat."

Alden followed him back to the kitchen and made him sit.

"You cooked. I hate to think you were on your feet that whole time."

"I was on one foot and my crutches. I cut the vegetables sitting down. I'm fine."

Alden dished the soup into bowls and sat next to Kit. "This is really sweet of you. Thank you."

"I'm sorry I pushed you to talk about something you didn't want to talk about."

"You didn't push; you just asked a question. I didn't mean to snap at you. There are things I can't talk about, because even thinking about them derails my entire day. My life before—" He shook his head. "I do feel safe with you. And this soup is really good."

"I'm glad." Kit smiled and took another sip of his own soup. "About you feeling safe with me."

"Who wouldn't? You're like two hundred fifty pounds of solid muscle. It's like having a mastiff in the house."

Kit wasn't sure what to say to that. On the one hand, Alden did love animals, so it was probably a compliment. On the other... "Did you just call me a dog?"

Alden nearly choked on his soup. "In a good way?"

This time, Kit didn't hold back his laughter, and before he knew it, Alden was laughing too. The tension that had hovered around the house since lunch time dissipated.

"I'm going to visit my mom tomorrow." Alden said, after the laughter died down. "Why don't you come with me?"

"Yeah?"

"She's dying to meet you. She asks me more about you than about me when I talk to her on the phone."

"Really?" That was strangely touching. Kit grinned. "I'd be happy to. I'm good with moms you know."

"You're good with everyone. It's disgusting, actually." Alden scowled again, but Kit could see laughter inside it. "I can hear her now. 'Why can't you be more like Kit? Kit says...'"

Kit balled up his napkin and threw it at Alden. "Stop it."

The fabric fell onto Alden's lap and Alden picked it up. "No, she'll love you. And Mr. Hendrick will, too. That's her neighbor she plays chess with. Well, she says they play chess, but I think they're fucking."

Kit nearly spit soup out of his nose, and Alden handed him his napkin back, then went back to eating as though nothing had happened.

After dinner, Alden insisted upon cleaning up and then surprised Kit by asking if he wanted to watch a movie.

"Sure. Um, what kind of movie?"

Alden shrugged. "You pick. But I like dance movies. And romantic comedies."

Kit raised an eyebrow, trying to figure out if Alden was pulling his leg. "Seriously?"

Alden nodded. "I'm okay with being a cliche. Have you *seen* the thighs on a ballet dancer?"

Laughing, Kit pulled up Netflix and started looking for something that fit the bill. He hadn't ever really considered a ballet dancer's thighs before, and clearly, he was missing out. As the opening credits scrolled onto the screen, he reached out and pulled Alden into a one-armed hug.

Alden froze up.

Oh man. Kit bit his lip. He hadn't meant to spook Alden. He felt so happy, and it was only natural for him to express it physically. He never would have thought twice about hugging most guys he'd been intimate with, but Alden was not most guys. As he tried to figure out how to play it off, Alden relaxed against him and pillowed his head on Kit's chest.

Well, that was—*different*. Kit gazed down at Alden in surprise. Was Alden Kaufman accepting affection? Without snark?

"Legs." Alden mumbled into his chest, and Kit looked back at the screen. Sure enough, a row of mens' legs filled the screen, dipping and kicking. They were long and slender and beautifully muscled. He could definitely see the appeal. They kind of reminded him of Alden's svelte runner's legs.

"Ballet dancers, huh?" Kit murmured back. "I think I get it."

TEN

Running was one of Alden's favorite self-soothing retreats. Like the brown noise, but better, because it was something he'd been doing for so long, he could relax into it as easily as breathing. The park was half a mile from his house, and it boasted a two-and-a-half-mile running path, so he could knock out three and half miles without even having to drive anywhere. He laced up his running shoes, tucked his earbuds into his ears, and let himself out the front door while Kit was still drinking overly sweet coffee at the kitchen table.

He fell into the rhythm of the run, thinking back to the night before. He'd been surprised when Kit pulled him into an embrace while they watched the ballet movie Kit had picked out, but after he got over the shock, he let himself enjoy it, just as he had when a sleepy Kit had rolled over and pulled him into an embrace while they were camping. But the cuddle hadn't progressed to anything more exciting, it hadn't lasted any longer than the movie, and it had left Alden disoriented and turned on. Had Kit been coming onto him and he'd missed it? Or was a cuddle just a cuddle?

He picked up the pace as he pondered whether hooking up

would be an epically stupid move while they were working and living together. Alden had never bothered to look at the employee handbook's fraternization policies, but he didn't think Dr. Evans would care, as long as it didn't affect their work. Besides, that ship had sailed anyway.

The idea of initiating something with Kit was confusing, in a way that it hadn't been on the mountain, when the kissing and the sex had clearly been about passing time and not about— feelings. But Alden had genuinely started to enjoy Kit's company, and that made everything more complicated. If he suggested hooking up and Kit turned him down, he'd be embarrassed and hurt. And he'd still have Kit hanging around for a few more weeks, which would be absolutely mortifying. And even if Kit didn't turn him down, if things went south, then they'd still be stuck with each other—unless Alden were to kick Kit out, which would be a real dick move, considering the guy was injured.

No. That wouldn't do. He'd just have to keep his hands to himself.

He could wait to see if Kit made a move, but frankly, he wasn't sure if he'd pick up on it unless Kit was a lot more direct about it than throwing an arm around him on the couch. And then what? No hurried hand job on the hillside. They'd have access to a bed, and all the time they needed to really enjoy each other.

He really needed to stop this train of thought. It wasn't going to happen, and he needed to stop trying to make it a possibility.

Resigned, he returned to the house to shower before he brought Kit to meet his mother. Maybe after she met Kit, she'd leave Alden alone and stop asking him questions about his temporary roommate.

He found Kit sprawled on the sofa, a book lying open on his chest, looking like he was ready to go back to sleep. "No sir, none of that," he called on his way down the hallway. "You need to be on your game when you meet my mama. That pretty smile of yours will only get you so far."

Kit's laughter followed him all the way to the bathroom.

———

Kit wasn't sure what to expect of the place where Alden's mom lived. Would it be like a hospital? He was well aware of how nervous hospitals made Alden. But it turned out to be more like a neighborhood. There were tidy, well-maintained yards, and the houses, while small, seemed nice, with front porches facing the sidewalk and orderly flowerbeds. Alden parked the Prius and raised an eyebrow at him.

"Ready?"

Kit grinned. "Absolutely. Bring it on."

Alden didn't knock on his mother's door, instead just opened it and walked in, calling out a greeting.

"Alden honey!" A woman's voice rang out, clearly happy to see her son. Kit made his way through the wide doorway and pulled the door closed behind him, balancing carefully. Alden had already rounded a corner into another room, so Kit followed to find Alden crouched next to a wheelchair, hugging the beautiful older woman who could only be his mother. Quicksilver gray-blue eyes met his over Alden's shoulder, and she smiled.

"You must be the fellow sleeping in my bed," she shook a finger at him. "Alden wasn't kidding—you're a giant."

Alden turned to face him, shrugging sheepishly, and Kit laughed. The two looked so much alike, with their blond hair and pale eyes.

"Christopher Taylor, ma'am." He held out his hand for a shake. "But everyone calls me Kit."

She clutched the offered hand and patted it between hers. "Brenda Kaufman. It's nice to meet you. Please sit down, I know those crutches can't be very comfortable. Alden, honey, why don't you put on a pot of coffee?"

"Yes, ma'am." Alden smiled indulgently at his mother, then left the room.

Kit settled himself onto her sofa, which was dainty and covered with flowers, and nowhere near as comfortable as the purple monstrosity in Alden's living room.

"How is he doing?" she asked almost immediately. "Is he taking his medicines?"

"As far as I know, he's good." Kit replied, puzzled. "Why do you ask?"

She shrugged. "I have a nurse who comes by once a day to make sure I'm doing what I'm supposed to, taking my medications and taking care of my prosthesis. He doesn't have anybody. I worry."

"Mom." Alden came into the room, scowling. "Kit is not going to spy on me for you, so drop it."

She shot Alden a fond glare. "Fine." Then she turned her attention back to Kit. "And why are you staying with my Alden? No family or girlfriend to take care of you? Don't men your age get married these days?"

Kit coughed to cover his surprise. "Maybe I will one day, Mrs. Kaufman. If I meet the right man."

A single eyebrow raised, and again he was stunned by the resemblance between her and her son. She glanced over at Alden, who was studying his fingernails as though they were the most fascinating thing he'd ever seen, then her gaze returned to Kit. "Are you dating my son, Kit?"

His face heated at the loaded question. Obviously, the answer was no—but it seemed wrong to deny there had been anything between the two of them right in front of the man. "No, ma'am."

"Well, why not? He's a catch. He was the salutatorian of his high school and still holds the school record in the 3200 meter. He also graduated Summa Cum Laude from Chapel Hill."

"Mom." Alden's voice sounded strangled. "You're embarrassing me in front of my friend."

"You're right, Mrs. Kaufman. He is a catch." Kit caught Alden's eye and smiled. "But we're friends. Colleagues. And he isn't sure he even likes me very much."

Alden blushed and fled the room, muttering something about the coffee.

"He does like you," she said quietly. "You wouldn't be in this house if he didn't. Or his house either. He's very protective of his personal space."

Kit looked down at his hands in his lap. "I like him too, ma'am." It was nothing but the truth, but it felt like a whispered confession. Like he was unburdening some small part of himself that he'd been keeping secret.

She promptly changed the subject. "When is your surgery?"

"My pre-op consultation is November third. They'll give me a definitive date then."

"It's so hard to get appointments with specialists this time of year. Everyone trying to get in before their deductibles reset." She frowned. "I hope you aren't in too much pain."

He smiled. "Only when I forget and try to stand on it."

"Try forgetting you only have one foot. I broke three ribs falling over myself in the dark." She winced. "It wasn't a good time."

"That's terrible."

She shrugged nonchalantly. "It was three years ago. My sugar was low, and I was disoriented. Now I have a pump, and my nurses. I don't have as many problems."

"Mom, can I help you into the recliner?" Alden asked as he came into the room with three steaming mugs. He set them on the coffee table, carefully arranging them on coasters.

She smiled. "If I wanted to be in the recliner, I'd already be in it."

Alden handed her a mug. "Be careful, it's hot. You're almost out of Splenda; do you need me to add some to your grocery order?"

She shook her head. "I've got more in the pantry."

Kit sat back and sipped the coffee, watching Alden coddle and care for his mom and listening to Alden describe the ballet movie they'd watched the night before.

"He was so tragically beautiful, Mom. He moved like Nureyev, and he was all cheekbones and broodiness. In the final scene, he was dancing on the beach alone after she left—" Alden clasped his hands over his heart. "—It was all I could do not to cry all over Kit's shoulder."

"It's streaming somewhere?" She pulled out her phone. "Let me get that title."

Kit had no idea Alden had been so affected by the movie. He himself had been riveted—but had chalked at least some of that up to being under Alden's spell. His closeness, the smell of his hair, the tiny movements of his body as he reacted to what he saw on the screen. Kit wouldn't have minded Alden crying on his shoulder and was a little disappointed he'd missed an opportunity to comfort him.

"What did you think of the movie?" She turned to Kit. "Did you like it as much as Alden did?"

"I thought the dancing looked really cool. But the plot was so sad. If Alden had started crying, I probably would have gotten choked up too."

Alden met his gaze, mouth open and soft. "Really?"

"I would have pretended I'd gotten something in my eyes."

Alden smiled. "Me too."

The rest of their visit, Alden kept looking at Kit, and Kit found he was having trouble not looking right back every time. Alden's attention on him was like a current of electricity humming over his skin and through his veins. When their eyes met, the current became a jolt.

Desire.

Kit couldn't deny that what he felt was deeper than attraction, warmer than friendship. It twisted and curled in him, building in intensity. But what the hell was he going to do with it?

In the car on the drive back to Alden's house, he stared out the window at nothing and everything, lost in his thoughts.

"She likes you." Alden said, and he stirred and looked across the car at his companion.

"I like her too."

"I'm sorry she was kind of pushy about the dating me thing. She knows I don't date."

"Why don't you date?" Kit asked, then realized it was almost certainly the agoraphobia.

Alden's face went soft and pensive. "I've thought for a long time it's because I'm too messed up. Like the dancer in the movie. Pushing people away."

"You aren't messed up." Kit took Alden's hand where it rested between them and gave it a gentle squeeze. "Just anxious. That's okay."

"Oh, I'm definitely messed up." Alden laughed bitterly. "Anxious is—not even scratching the surface. But thank you for trying to cheer me up."

Alden very carefully extricated his hand from Kit's and placed it back on the steering wheel. They didn't speak again for the rest of the drive.

That evening, Alden ate dinner in his office with the door

closed, even though it was Saturday. Kit knew, deep down, he wouldn't have said or done anything differently, but the closed door hurt his feelings anyway. Alden needed his space, and Kit respected that, but the idea that Alden needed to be away from him, specifically? That cut deeply.

When the door opened and Alden emerged, it was nearly ten o'clock. He wandered through the living room with his earbuds in, carrying his dirty dishes, and didn't seem to notice Kit sitting on the sofa.

"Hey," Kit called out softly, and Alden jumped, then pulled the earbuds out. When he turned to face Kit, his eyes were red and puffy, which made them look bluer than ever.

"Hey."

"I put the leftovers away. Did you get enough to eat?"

Alden nodded. "Yeah, thanks. I'm sorry I got so weird this afternoon. I get in these moods sometimes." He shrugged helplessly.

"S'okay." Kit hefted himself off the couch, grabbing his crutches. He followed Alden into the kitchen. "I'm guessing you absolutely don't want to talk about it?"

Alden gave him a tiny smile over his shoulder. "You're guessing right."

In the kitchen, Kit maneuvered so that he could get a better look at Alden's eyes. He'd definitely been crying. "Are you okay?"

"I'm fine. It's nothing."

"You've been crying."

"You shouldn't notice things like that."

"I'm observant. One of the things that makes me good at my job."

"I got something in my eye," Alden said flatly.

"Something like depression?"

"For fuck's sake, Kit, I'm exhausted and I don't want to talk about my feelings. Go to bed, okay? I'll be just normal-grumpy by morning, I promise."

"Okay." Kit let it drop, even though he wanted nothing more than to pull Alden into his arms and hold him until whatever was hurting him stopped. "I'm here if you need anything."

This time when Alden smiled, his whole face softened. "I know. Thank you."

Kit made his way back to the bedroom, carrying the image of that smile with him. The fact that Alden's retreat to his office to cry wasn't about him was a relief, but the fact that he'd needed to do it at all was troubling. Kit wasn't sure he'd ever truly know the undercurrents of Alden's emotional states, but even after the rollercoaster of today, he wanted to.

Alden woke to the sound of voices—familiar voices that didn't make sense together. Kit, laughing, and... *Tommy?*

He sat up in bed. He smelled coffee but not cigarettes, so Tommy couldn't have been here long. Oh, dear God. What the hell was he going to do with Tommy? Could his timing be any worse? And how was he going to explain Tommy just showing up here to Kit?

Another of Kit's laughs floated down the hall, but Alden couldn't make out what either of them were saying. What a goddamn disaster.

He took a deep breath and looked for his slippers. He could do this. Once Tommy realized Alden had a houseguest, he wouldn't expect to stay. And once he was gone, Alden could explain—well, why should he have to explain anything? His arrangement with Tommy just made him seem more pathetic than ever. And Kit had just caught him crying last night.

Shit—what if Kit thought Alden *invited* Tommy? This could not be happening. No.

Alden tried to look casual as he walked into the living room, even though his heart was beating a million times a minute and felt like it would explode out of his chest.

"Good morning." He looked around. Kit was on the couch, with the phone to his ear, laughing. And Tommy was nowhere to be seen. Had he been dreaming?

"Hey, there's coffee in the pot." Kit grinned at him, then "No, that's the guy I'm staying with. Yeah. His name's Alden, and we work together. Hey, the show's coming back on. Yeah. Okay, I'll be quiet." He laughed again.

Alden glanced over his shoulder at the TV, and immediately felt like an idiot.

Science Sunday starring Tommy Nguyen was on. Because of course Kit would watch a science show for little kids. He watched for a moment as the Tommy on the screen stuck his hands into a compost tumbler and pulled out a handful of nearly black compost.

"And that's how we use the waste from our kitchens to grow more food. Isn't science cool?"

Alden snorted. Tommy hamming it up for the camera was very different from the Tommy he'd known for over decade. In real life, Tommy was intense and jaded. But somehow, on television? The excited "Isn't science cool?" act really worked.

He made his way to the kitchen, poured himself a cup of coffee, and joined Kit on the couch. They watched as Tommy tilled compost into a garden, explaining how it added nutrients to the soil in terms even a small child could understand. Kit guffawed at something the person on the phone said.

"Okay, tell your mom and dad and ZoZo that I love them. I'll talk to you next week. Love you too." He hung up and looked at

Alden. "I'm so sorry, I didn't mean to wake you up. I try to watch *Science Sunday* with Abigail whenever I can."

Abigail. Oh, the niece with the frog.

"Your niece?"

Kit nodded. "How are you feeling this morning?

Relieved that Tommy Nguyen isn't actually standing in his living room, but Alden wasn't about to say it.

"I'm fine. Thanks for the coffee."

Kit smiled over his own mug and muted Tommy on the television. "I know it's a silly show, but Abby really likes it, and I try to encourage all of her science-related interests."

"It's not silly. Tommy can explain the nitrogen cycle in terms a six-year-old can understand. That's a skill set."

Kit nodded. "I like that there are shows like this that Abigail can watch and ask me questions about what I do. Although today she only wanted to talk about you."

"Me? Why?"

"Because I'm in your house, and she thinks I've got a secret boyfriend. She's six. Where do kids come up with this stuff?" Kit shook his head. "She's every bit as nosy as your mom. We can't let them ever meet."

Alden smiled at that. When on earth would his mom meet Kit's family? "So, you're saying she's six going on sixty?"

"And who knows what she's overhearing my sister say. Anyway, she had to get dressed for Sunday school, so I didn't have to explain how an anterior cruciate ligament works and that it's not something someone could kiss better."

Alden smiled at that. If he were another kind of man, he'd arch an eyebrow and offer to give it a try.

But he wasn't that kind of man, was he?

ELEVEN

Alden scrubbed a hand over his eyes as the numbers blurred on the screen. There were holes in the data—whether because the researchers hadn't observed everything they had planned, or because they hadn't recorded it properly, or because the scope of the research had changed, he didn't know. He hadn't read the email that had come with the report, and now he was annoyed. And hungry.

Kit had made popcorn. The smell was driving Alden crazy—no microwave popcorn with that awful fake butter, but the real stuff. Kettle-popped. Kit had commandeered Alden's favorite saucepan for popcorn use a few days after he moved in, and now Alden was a convert.

His lips curled up in a smile as he remembered Kit crowing with joy when he figured out how to balance on one crutch and shake the saucepan over the stove. He'd looked so sexy that day, filling Alden's kitchen with his big body, thick mountain-man legs bulging under gray sweatpants. Alden had wanted to jump him where he stood.

Alden's dick was getting hard just remembering it—they did say smell was the sense most tied to memory. Would he ever smell popcorn again without springing wood? He rubbed his eyes again and glared at the numbers on the screen. He could take a break. Kit was probably stretched out on the couch with a bowl of popcorn. Maybe Alden could join him and wrangle a good cuddle out of it—maybe even the kind that led to a hand job. Oh, for fuck's sake. Why was this so hard? They'd already had sex. Why couldn't he just suggest they do it again? Living in each other's pockets was driving him crazy.

No. He wanted popcorn. Not a hand job. Okay, so he pretty much could always go for a hand job, but he and Kit were room-mates right now, not—boyfriends. Not lovers. This was a prac-tical arrangement and not one it would be fair to fuck up just because he couldn't stop thinking about Kit's body in those sweatpants. And how annoying was it that he was still having this conversation with himself on a near-daily basis?

He turned off the monitor and tugged the earbuds out of his ears, immediately missing the soothing brown noise. Through the wall, muffled voices rumbled. Kit must be watching a movie, which meant Alden had worked through dinner again. Damn.

He stood and stretched, his back popping as the bunched-up muscles in his shoulders let go of some of their tension. It felt *good* to get out of his chair. He grabbed his coffee mug and the plate that had held his lunch off the desk and started for the kitchen.

When he opened the door to his office, gunfire filled the house.

He hit the floor, shaking with terror. Pain shot through his left hand—was he hit? He covered his ears, trying to block out the screams. Blood trickled down his face and the smell of it made him retch.

The popping sound of gunfire disappeared, and he realized he was the one screaming.

"What the hell—Alden?"

A loud crash sounded from the hallway, then frantic, tortured screaming filled the house. *Alden.*

The sound was one of raw terror, unlike anything Kit had ever heard before. All thoughts vanished besides one—he had to get to Alden. He grabbed for his crutches, dropping one. "Goddamn it!"

He left it on the floor, unable to think of anything beyond getting to Alden and fixing whatever was making him scream. Was this a panic attack? Is this why Alden didn't want to go out in public? He used the one crutch to bear his weight as he hopped around the corner.

Alden was face down on the floor, hands over his ears, screaming and retching. A plate and mug lay broken on the floor next to him and blood was dripping from one of his hands. His eyes were clenched tightly shut.

"What the hell—Alden?" Kit tossed the crutch to the side and slid down the wall to the floor. "Alden, baby, you're safe. You're safe. It's okay." He slowly reached out and laid a gentle hand on Alden's shaking shoulder. Alden twitched violently, but he stopped screaming and took in a rough breath.

Kit rubbed at Alden's shoulder. "Hey. You're safe. It's okay." He repeated the words over and over as Alden's eyes focused and his shallow, panicked breaths seemed to slow and deepen.

"I've been shot."

Shot? Kit grabbed Alden's bloody hand. A deep gash scored the inside of his palm, but it didn't look anything like a gunshot wound—more like he'd been cut by the shattered plate on the floor.

"It's just a cut, baby. How about we get off the floor and I'll clean it up for you?"

"Are they gone?"

"Are who gone?"

Alden moaned and started dry heaving again. Unsure of what to do or how to handle what appeared to be some kind of psychotic break, Kit rubbed Alden's back and kept repeating that he was safe, he was home, and no one was there but the two of them. When Alden stopped heaving, Kit pulled off his own shirt and bandaged Alden's hand with it. He managed to get Alden to a sitting position, and Alden moved into his lap, docile as a kitten.

Kit wrapped both arms around him and rubbed his hands everywhere he could reach on Alden's sweaty, trembling body.

"Are you okay?"

Alden didn't speak. He buried his face in Kit's shoulder and clung to him.

"I can't pick you up, babe. Do you think you can get to your bedroom?" Alden shuddered in his arms.

"I'm home?"

Kit sucked in a relieved breath. "Yeah. You're home, and I've got you. You haven't been shot, and there's no one else here. If you can get to your bedroom, I'll clean up your hand and tuck you in, and then we'll talk, okay?"

"Kit?" Alden looked around the hallway, and then at him with wide blue eyes, finally seeming clear and focused.

"Yeah. It's me. Can you walk?"

Something seemed to harden in Alden's face, and he stood up, then reached down his good hand to help Kit. Grateful for the help, even though it felt like it should be the other way around, Kit used Alden's counterbalance and the wall to haul himself upright. As soon as he was up, Alden dropped his hand and picked up the crutch.

"I have to clean this up." Alden spoke woodenly, not looking at Kit as he handed the crutch to him.

"It can wait. Let's get you into bed and let me have a look at your hand, okay?"

"I'm fine. It was a flashback. I had a flashback, and I'll be fine."

"A flashback to what?" What part of Alden's life history had Kit missed?

Alden looked at Kit, surprise written all over his face. "I thought you knew. I thought everybody at work knew. It was winter break. I was home from grad school to spend the holidays with my parents. My dad and I were at Northridge Mall shopping for last minute gifts when—" Alden swallowed and then dropped to his knees and started picking up the shattered pieces of stoneware and piling them on top of the largest piece. "This was my favorite mug."

Kit reeled back, bracing himself against the wall, and struggling to suck in a breath. The massacre at Northridge Mall had dominated both the local and national news. A gunman had opened fire in the food court, killing his ex-girlfriend and nine bystanders, and wounding a dozen more before turning the gun on himself. "Your dad died when you were in grad school—oh God—That's how he died? And you were there?"

Alden flinched, but he didn't stand up or look at Kit. "I have to clean up this mess. Please don't watch violent movies in my house again."

―――――――

Of course, Alden didn't expect Kit to leave it at that—why would he? But Alden needed space to calm his fraying nerves.

"Alden, I'm so sorry. I didn't know."

He took a deep breath. "I understand that. Now that you know, we can avoid any further potentially triggering events."

"Is this why you were crying the other night? Is this what—"

Alden dropped the handle of the cup on top of the pile and shook his head.

"Kit. Please. Give me some goddamn space. That was—terrifying and humiliating, and I can't do anything about the fact that you saw me cowering in the hallway screaming, but I can do something about the broken shit on the floor. Let me have a little dignity, okay?"

Kit stood there, all hulking and gorgeous, a living, breathing reminder that Alden couldn't have nice things. He let out a sigh and asked softly, "What can I do?"

Alden closed his eyes and swallowed back tears. "Run a bath? Make some tea? I don't give a fuck."

Kit laughed. "Do you even drink tea?"

Alden felt the smile tugging at his lips even as the first tears started spilling out of his eyes. "No."

"I guess I'll go make myself some tea, then."

"You do that."

He listened to Kit hobble off toward the kitchen on his single crutch, and then he let the shaking take over his body. He'd learned a long time ago that the grief would catch up after the flashbacks. And he'd probably have trouble sleeping if he didn't take a Xanax before bed. But he would deal with that later. For now, he collected the pieces of stoneware off the floor with shaking hands and concentrated on taking slow, even breaths, until he could stand up without crying.

When he got to the kitchen, two steaming mugs of tea sat on the table, and Kit stood leaning against the counter with his arms folded over his chest and the crutches propped up next to him.

"It's herbal. It won't keep you up."

"Thanks." Alden dumped the broken stoneware in the garbage and picked up one of the mugs. His hands were shaking and tea splashed out onto the floor as he raised it to his mouth.

"Come here." Kit reached out and tugged Alden's sweater, pulling him close. He took the mug from Alden's hands and set it aside, then wrapped both arms around Alden and *hugged* him.

The shaking intensified, and Alden had just a moment to wonder if maybe he wasn't all right after all before Kit's hands started rubbing up and down his arms. Alden buried his face in Kit's chest and sucked in a deep lungful of air that smelled like his mountain man.

"Are you hungry?" Kit didn't stop rubbing, but now he seemed to be petting Alden all over, running his hands over his back and his shoulders and even the back of his head. Alden sank into those touches, clinging to Kit's waist and closing his eyes and just letting the novelty of human touch soothe him.

"Babe. Hungry?" Kit prodded.

Alden shook his head. He had been, but now he had Kit's hands on him and that was so much better than food. "You called me babe."

"Yeah. I'm sorry. Once I've been intimate with someone, it's hard to go back to—well. You know. I'll try not to."

"I like it." Alden murmured. "No one calls me nice things."

The noise Kit let out then was a broken little huff, like he was mad that no one had nice nicknames for Alden, but who would? Alden smiled against the soft thermal covering Kit's chest. "But I like 'sasshole' better."

Kit's rumbling laugh shook Alden's body too, and it felt good, like cuddling a purring cat, and Alden found himself saying "Let's get a cat."

"Better idea: Let's get you cleaned up and into bed."

First, Kit made Alden sit at the table and hold out his hand for inspection. The cut wasn't deep, and the bleeding had stopped, so Kit cleaned it and covered it with an oversized Band-Aid. Then Kit used his crutch to nudge him off toward the bedroom with both mugs of tea and followed him there.

Kit sat on the bed and sipped his tea as Alden got undressed, watching with a wary expression. Alden tossed his clothes in the hamper and pulled on a pair of shorts to sleep in, and Kit just stared like he thought Alden was going to start screaming again any second.

"I can put myself to bed."

"I know. But I kind of want to be near you right now." Kit shrugged. "It's stupid, right? But hearing you scream like that—"

Alden's face got hot. "Don't remind me."

"Shut up, I'm serious. It scared the shit out of me. I need to see you're okay. I don't understand why, because this is totally selfish of me, and I'm not usually that clingy kind of person, but I just want some reassurance."

"Be reassured." Alden picked up the bottle of paroxetine from his dresser and took his nightly dose. Then he grabbed the bottle of Xanax next to it and took one of those too before crawling into bed. "I'm fine. When I have trouble sleeping, I know where to find my sleeping pills."

Kit stretched out next to him. "Can I sleep in here with you?"

"Seriously?"

"Yeah."

"Your leg?"

"I'll be okay."

Kit's face was so open and soft and needy, and Alden couldn't believe he was agreeing to this, because damn it, he was the one who'd just been traumatized, but it was Kit who was begging for comfort. Or to be allowed to comfort. Alden wasn't sure which. But the oh-so-bad-idea of spending the night in Kit's arms was far too appealing to reject.

"Okay," he agreed.

Alden listened to the rustling noises of Kit getting ready for bed and then sliding under the blankets beside him. The light blinked out. He thought that would be that, but then Kit reached out and hauled him up against that big muscly body, burying a hand in his hair. Alden sucked in a breath.

"Is this okay?" Kit whispered into the dark.

Alden nodded, and then the tension went out of Kit's body. The hand in Alden's hair started stroking, and Alden let out the breath and snuggled closer, wrapping his own hand around Kit's waist. Kit made a pleased noise and pressed a kiss onto Alden's forehead.

"This isn't exactly platonic cuddling," Alden muttered against Kit's chest.

"It's totally platonic if you ignore my hard-on."

Alden laughed and squeezed Kit a little tighter.

"How do you do this to me?" Kit's voice was full of wonder. "How do you make me joke and laugh not an hour after..."

When it was clear Kit wasn't going to finish that sentence, Alden shrugged. "You make me laugh too. I guess... I guess it's a thing friends do."

"Is that what we are? Cause I like that."

"Me too."

"Alden, were you hurt that day? When your dad was—"

"Yes, but I don't remember that part."

"You're okay now, though?

Alden yawned, letting the heat from Kit's body warm him through. "Physically, I'm fine. Emotionally, mentally? I'm a mess. I have PTSD. Agoraphobia. Flashbacks that feel like hallucinations. Difficulty with intimacy."

"Intimacy—you mean sex?"

"No. My dick works fine. It's my brain—and my mouth—that's the problem."

"You push people away."

Alden sighed. "It's more complicated than that. I sabotage relationships. I don't trust easily, and I don't spend enough time with people to let my guard down and get to know someone. My therapist says it's part of my trauma response, and I can get better at it if I work on it, but why bother? Who is ever going to want this?" He gestured frustratingly at himself in the dark, and Kit grabbed his hand and held it in his own.

"Don't talk about yourself like that."

Why not? Alden fought the urge to push away. The calming effect of the Xanax had started to settle through him, and fighting with Kit felt like too much work.

"I've never known anyone who's been shot before." Kit finally said. "I'm sorry that happened to you."

Alden snuggled closer to Kit, who still clung to his hand. "Thank you for being here tonight." He yawned. "No one has ever stuck around after one of those."

Kit made a rough, wordless noise and squeezed him tighter. Alden tried to think of something more to say, but sleep was pulling him down, and he drifted off in silence.

TWELVE

Alden woke to two hundred and fifty pounds of mountain man wrapped around him like a warm weighted blanket. He took in a deep breath and snuggled closer. He'd had plenty of time to sneak glances at Kit's body over the last weeks, but they'd paced around each other at a distance—wary of repeating the intimacy they'd shared in the rainy tent on their aborted hiking trip. To be close enough to feel Kit's heartbeat was a treat he wanted to savor.

"You awake?" Kit's voice rumbled through his chest, vibrating right through Alden.

"Yeah." Alden started to pull away, but Kit hauled him right back.

"Stay."

"I don't need pity." Alden pushed this time, sitting up into the cold morning air. "I got enough of that last night."

"I'm not offering any pity." Kit sat up and scowled. "Why does this have to be so hard? I like you; I think you're sexy, and I really want to kiss you, but I wasn't going to put the moves on you while you were sleeping."

Alden blinked slowly, staring at Kit as the scowl turned into a soft smile. His curly brown hair was tousled and his chin was stubbled, but the look in his eyes was one hundred percent seduction. Alden flushed, dropping his gaze, which made him blush even harder because Kit's body truly was magnificent.

"I'm sorry. I ruin everything." Alden looked away.

"I'm not going to let you ruin this." Kit put his hand on Alden's knee and squeezed. "Look at me."

Alden looked. Kit's face was soft and open, his grin reaching all the way to his eyes. His hand drifted from Alden's knee to his chin, and Alden wanted to rub his face into that palm.

"I can't promise you anything. I'm not the kind of guy who makes attachments." Kit's thumb traced the cleft in Alden's chin, then glided over his bottom lip. "But I like you, sasshole. I like how prickly you are, even. I like that you're making me spell out my intentions. So here it is: I want you. I've been thinking about that mutual hand job in the woods so much it feels like an obsession. Your voice haunts my dreams. Neither one of us is in a relationship, and we have great chemistry. Why can't we just enjoy that without any strings?"

Alden swallowed, his eyes drifting closed. *Attachments. Intentions. Obsession. Haunts.* These weren't the words one used to propose a friendship with benefits. They were too much, too strong, too raw. Was Kit lying to Alden or himself? And what did it matter, when the offer was this sweet? No strings attached. Just to enjoy their great chemistry. Yes, that could be enough for Alden. Couldn't it?

He leaned forward, not breaking eye contact until the last possible second. Kit held breathlessly still until their lips connected, a tiny, soft collision sending a shock wave through both of them. What started as a question turned into an urgency firing in Alden's belly. He deepened the kiss, holding Kit's stubbled chin and plundering his mouth.

Kit seemed more than content to let Alden lead, so he straddled Kit's lap and sank one hand into those wildly messy curls. Kit let out a soft moan, and Alden tightened his grip.

It was dizzyingly perfect. Alden was fully hard, and he pushed down at his shorts to let the tip of his dick free

Their hips pushed together, mimicking the give and take of their kiss. Kit reached up and danced his fingers across Alden's cheekbone, then slid them down to tug Alden closer.

Heat licked up Alden's spine as he ground down on Kit. He pulled back, dragging a rough breath into his lungs. "This is messy," he warned.

"It doesn't have to be." Kit captured his lips again, then eased away. "We can keep it simple."

Alden's eyes drifted closed again as Kit's mouth and hands worked a slow magic. Before long he was rolling his hips with utter abandon, lost in a haze of pleasure.

Alden's roaming hands re-discovered textures, mapping Kit's body. The hot silk of skin, the soft tickle of hair, the hard pebble of a nipple. When clothes got in the way, they were pulled off and tossed aside until both were naked and breathless. "How do you want to do this?" Alden nudged Kit with a knee as he moved over him.

"I want whatever you want." Kit grinned back at him. "But I can't stop thinking about what you said in the woods."

Alden smiled, shameless and powerful, two things he wasn't used to feeling. "The part about you blowing me?" He palmed his cock and gave it a long slow stroke. Kit's eyes followed every move. "Or the part about me fucking you?"

Kit shivered, catching his lower lip between his teeth. "Please?"

Alden caught Kit's lips in another kiss, reaching between them to stroke Kit's cock. It was large, uncut, and gorgeous. He pushed the skin back, then pulled it forward again, watching the way Kit's breathing changed, awestruck. This giant of a man, at his mercy, letting him lead. When he was younger, too many men had seen Alden's slight form and taken that as permission to push him around in bed. He didn't want that, but he hadn't expected *this*. Kit was impossibly perfect. Alden ran his thumb around the wet tip of Kit's cock, watching Kit grow more excited with every pass.

"Roll over." He sat back on his heels and watched Kit move, graceful for such a large man, careful to accommodate his injured knee as he came to rest on his stomach, glancing over his shoulder.

"Be gentle, sasshole, I haven't done this in a while."

Alden smiled at the nickname, then climbed over Kit to claim a messy, frantic kiss. How was this so good? He lined his body up over Kit, pressing his cock against the crevice of Kit's ass and rocking gently until Kit broke the kiss and pushed back into him.

He slid his way down Kit's body, pressing kisses down the length of his spine, biting gently at the swell of a buttock, then pushing insistently at his massive right thigh until Kit slid it forward, putting himself on display for Alden, hinting wordlessly at what they both needed.

He stroked his thumb lightly over Kit's hole, feeling the way Kit shivered and clenched in excitement. He leaned in, licking gently, then more firmly, as Kit began to rock back and forth and make low, excited noises. When he added a finger, Kit bucked forward, then pushed back, letting out a broken groan.

"Alden—" he whispered, practically humping the sheets.

"Mmmm?" Alden hummed.

"Please. Fucking *please*."

"Your knee?" he asked softly.

"Is fine," Kit practically growled. "Please."

And how could he say no to that? He grabbed a condom and a bottle of lube from the drawer by the bed and sheathed himself quickly. But this wasn't right. He wanted—no *needed*—to see Kit's face while they did this.

"Roll over," he said again, helping Kit return to his back, then taking his fill of another dizzying kiss. He didn't want to rush any part of this.

He coated his fingertips with lube and then pushed at Kit's rim, making him slick and wet. Something about the sight of his fingertips dipping in and out of that hot hole was mesmerizing. Every time he pulled out, Kit rocked his hips, chasing fingers. How amazing would that feel on Alden's dick? He couldn't get enough of teasing Kit, watching his reactions as he slowly fell apart. His breath caught when Kit started thrusting into the air, and he couldn't wait a moment longer, not even to tease Kit. Alden covered his own dick with lube, then tossed the bottle aside and lined himself up. He kissed Kit's shoulder.

"Ready?"

"Please," Kit repeated. "*Please.*"

Alden tried to push in gently, to go slowly, but Kit was wild with lust, shoving himself onto Alden's dick and letting out a ragged hiss.

"Fuck!"

"Okay?" Alden murmured, kissing Kit's chest and holding as still as possible even though every instinct in him urged to drive forward, to fuck into the tight heat of Kit's body. He was caught in a storm of desire, frantic to move and yet desperate to make it last forever.

Slowly, slowly, Kit relaxed, rocking side to side and taking Alden deeper. He let out a rough breath as he rose up on his elbows and ground down on Alden's dick.

It was too much, too hot, too good. Alden moaned and pushed all the way home. "Fuck, Kit. You feel so good."

He rocked into Kit's impossibly perfect body, and Kit responded by pushing back, giving as good as he got. When

Alden ground forward, he could tell the exact moment he hit Kit's gland by the way Kit shivered and whined. He pulled back and did it again, and again, pulling more desperate, delicious cries from Kit.

He was going to lose his mind right here in this bed, with this man, and the whole experience was so unbelievably hot he couldn't begin to care if there wasn't anything left of him when it was done. He slid a hand between their bodies, gripping Kit's cock and jerking it roughly as he drove into him again and again.

"I'm gonna come, Ald—ah!" Kit shouted as Alden thrust forward. "Alden, now, babe." Alden sped his hand up, losing the rhythm with his hips for a moment, but it didn't matter because Kit's gorgeous face contorted as he cried out. Come coated Alden's hand, hot and slick, and Kit's whole body seized up with ecstasy. Alden drove into him harder, losing himself in tight heat, pleasure surging in him until it exploded. He shuddered as he pushed himself into Kit's body one last time.

"Oh my God." He pulled out slowly, using the last remaining bit of sense in his head to remove the condom and toss it into the wastebasket. "Kit, oh my God."

Kit reached up, his face and chest flushed and sweaty as he pulled Alden into another kiss. Alden sank down onto Kit's body, and the kiss was sweet and sticky and perfect.

"That was so good," Kit murmured. "I haven't done that in so long, thank you."

"You were so beautiful." Alden trailed kisses along Kit's jaw to whisper in his ear, "I wish it could have lasted forever."

"We can do it again," Kit yawned and stretched. "But right now, my knee hurts like a sonofabitch."

Alden winced, ashamed. Had some of those noises he thought were excitement been pain? "I'm sorry. I was too rough."

"It was fine. I'm not made of glass. And the way you made me feel just now was absolutely worth it."

"I'm sorry."

"Stop apologizing. You didn't do anything I didn't want. That was fucking awesome."

"I'll make breakfast." Alden pushed himself up and started glancing around for his underwear.

"Wait." Kit pulled him back down and kissed him, deep and slow, rekindling the heat in Alden's gut. "Don't run away from this."

"I'm not." But it was a lie. Alden couldn't meet Kit's gaze until Kit cupped his chin and lifted. "I'm not. I just want to take care of you."

"Liar." Kit smiled. "But breakfast sounds good."

Alden managed a weak smile in return. "I'll make French toast."

"Sounds great."

He grabbed his underwear and made a quick exit to the bathroom, where he washed up and tried to hold back the rush of feelings threatening to overwhelm him. Kit was one of the hottest men he'd ever met in his life, and he seemed to have an endless well of affection and giving in his soul. How was Alden supposed to escape from this no-strings entanglement with his heart intact?

Kit wasn't going to let Alden disappear into his shell again. Not after last night.

Not after this morning.

Thinking about Alden's hands on his body could reignite him instantly. He liked bottoming, liked it a lot, but there was something *more* about the way Alden touched him—bossy and reverent together—that made everything hotter.

He showered as quickly as possible, and then threw on his robe and made his way to the kitchen. Alden was still mostly naked, but in a nod to kitchen safety, had pulled on an apron. His ass in those tight white briefs flexed as he walked around the kitchen, and the sight made Kit's body take notice. So fucking hot. And he didn't even seem to know it.

"Hey," he said from the doorway.

"Hey, yourself." Alden called over his shoulder. "I made coffee. Come and get it."

Kit crossed the room and planted a kiss on Alden's shoulder, running his fingertips down Alden's arm. "Thank you." As his fingertips ran back up to Alden's shoulder, they stopped at a rough ridge of flesh. He glanced down at where his fingers stroked over the octopus tattoo, halfway between shoulder and elbow. Scar tissue, ridges and whorls of it, was hidden in the curves and coils of the tentacle. "Is this—?"

Alden shuddered and spoke woodenly. "Gunshot wounds leave scars."

"Does it hurt when I touch it?"

Alden shook his head. "It feels different than the rest of my skin, but no, it doesn't hurt."

Kit balanced precariously on his crutches and leaned down to kiss the knotted skin. "I never would have seen it under that tattoo."

"That's sort of the idea."

"You're such a brave man." Kit murmured, kissing the scar again. "You've survived so much. And you're still here."

Alden's spatula clattered down onto the floor. "Please don't."

"Don't what? Don't touch your scars?" Kit drew back, confused.

"Don't act like survival is some grand achievement. Don't act like most of me didn't die in that food court with my dad. I'm *not* brave. I'm terrified to leave my house."

Alden's voice was cold and sharp. That wouldn't do. Kit turned him around, wrapping one of his arms around Alden's waist as he did. Two circles of color sat high on Alden's cheekbones, and tears glittered wetly in his eyes.

"Don't," he whispered.

Kit held him gently and pressed a kiss to his forehead. "You're brave *because* you're terrified and you keep going. Every time you step out of your house, it's a miracle."

Alden shook his head. "Don't," he whispered again.

Kit kissed him as tenderly as he could, wiping the tears away from Alden's eyes. "You're brave to let me see this, and I won't let you push me away. I won't let you sabotage our friendship."

"Don't." Alden barely breathed the word as his arms came up and around Kit's neck. "Don't let me ruin this."

Kit turned off the burner on the stove.

It was a long time and another shower later, this time together, before they salvaged the French toast.

THIRTEEN

Kit's surgery date loomed on the calendar, and neither of them seemed willing to talk about it. Sure, they made oblique references to "when you go back to the office" or "I'll bet you'll be glad to have your place to yourself again," but they never really dug beneath the surface. But the evening after Kit's pre-op appointment, Alden finally decided to man up and address the situation head on.

"Do you need me to drive you and pick you up from your surgery appointment on Thursday?" he asked as he ladled soup into bowls over the stove.

"My mom has offered to come do it," Kit answered gruffly, cutting bread and not making eye contact. "I know how much you hate hospitals."

"Oh." Alden tried to cover his disappointment with a too-bright tone. "I guess that's good, then."

"I haven't told her yes yet. I was going to call her tonight."

"She doesn't have to drive all this way—I can do it." Alden took a deep breath. "I want to do it. For you."

Kit looked up at him then, eyes wide. "Really?"

Alden nodded, his stomach churning with nerves. "I feel—" He stopped. He felt too much of everything. Like he would die if he wasn't the first person to touch Kit after surgery. Like he'd rather cut off his own arm than let Kit go through this without him. Like there wasn't enough Xanax in the world to make him comfortable in a hospital, but fuck being comfortable, he'd rather be with Kit. "—I feel responsible," he finished lamely.

"Oh." Kit looked back down at the cutting board. "You're not, though. And I'm sure you have work."

"Kit, just let me fucking drive you, okay?" Alden burst out. "I want to be there for you."

Kit's eyebrows drew together. "Okay. Fine."

"Fine."

But it wasn't fine. Kit didn't tease Alden over dinner, and he disappeared into his room as soon as the dishes were done. He was clearly annoyed with Alden, and Alden didn't have the words to bridge the chasm yawning between them. Finally, he called his own mother.

"Alden, honey."

He smiled. "Hi, Mom."

"How are you? How's Kit doing?"

"I'm good. Kit's good. He's got surgery Thursday."

"Oh, that's wonderful. I know he'll be so glad to be able to walk by Thanksgiving. Well, maybe. I've been Googling about his recovery time."

Yeah, Kit had Alden's mom completely charmed. "Speaking of Thanksgiving—I know we haven't talked to your doctor about it yet, but do you think you can come over for dinner? You can stay for the weekend, even."

"And put Kit out of his bedroom? Oh honey, I couldn't."

"It's *your* bedroom, Mom. He can bunk in with me. If he's even still here. Like you said, he might be walking by then."

"Well, that just wouldn't be right." He could practically hear her shaking her head.

"Mom."

"Well, you're both gay. It wouldn't be right."

"I'm not going to speak in euphemisms here." Alden took a deep breath. "You're right, we're both gay. We're also grown-ass adults. We're living in each other's pockets, and I need you to believe me and not ask questions that will embarrass us both when I tell you there's nothing that could happen between Kit and me that hasn't already. Okay? I don't want to miss out on spending Thanksgiving with you because you're concerned for my nonexistent virtue."

"Alden!"

"Mom."

"You both told me you were just friends."

"We are just friends." Alden pinched the bridge of his nose and tried to remember that at least she was acknowledging he was gay. This was progress. "Sometimes friends do stuff and it's just friendly. You know that's true for men and women too, so I don't understand what the big deal is."

"I don't understand why you would characterize a sexual relationship with someone you obviously have feelings for as just friends." She huffed.

"It's not those kinds of feelings," he lied. "Friendship with a side of pants-feelings is not love."

"Friendship with a side of pants-feelings is what used to be called marriage, honey."

And Alden didn't have anything to say to that. "I'm calling your doctor tomorrow."

"Have you even asked Kit if he wants me there?"

Don't swear, don't swear, don't swear.

"Mom. I want you here. I do. Your son. I want to roast a

turkey and fix all the sides and remind you to check your sugars and spoil you for the day. *I* want you here. What is the problem?"

"Marie was going to come visit me," she confessed after a long silence.

Marie. Her sister, who was a self-righteous bitch. Alden didn't want her in his house, but if that's what it took to get his mom home for the holiday, that's what it took. He was totally capable of compromise.

"Aunt Marie can come too. And if she gives you a ride, that solves the whole bedroom problem."

"Really, Alden?" He could hear the happiness in her voice, and even though the idea of having Aunt Marie at his table bothered him, at least it would make his mother happy.

The conversation ended shortly after that, and he stood and went to knock on Kit's bedroom door.

"Yeah, come in."

"You decent? I hope not." He covered his eyes with one hand and pushed the door open. When he dropped the hand, he saw Kit sprawled on the bed in nothing but his boxers and his knee brace with the most recent novel of the psychic cop series—he was totally addicted now—in one hand. "Hey."

"Hey." Kit smiled up at him. "I'm sorry I was testy with you earlier. I'm nervous about Thursday. I shouldn't have taken it out on you."

Alden's shoulders dropped in relief, and he crawled onto the bed beside Kit and cuddled into his shoulder. "No, I should have been more sensitive in how I brought it up. I should have offered instead of asking if you needed a ride. It was badly worded. I'm not good at people-stuff."

"I appreciate that you're willing to do this. I think Mom was disappointed when I told her I didn't need her to come. You know how it is. I'm a grown man, but I'm her youngest kid so she still wants to baby me."

Alden smiled. "Who could blame her when she's got the sweetest son ever?"

"Stop, that sounded like a compliment. What happened to my sasshole?"

"Oh, he's still here. Listen, I know you might be on your feet by Thanksgiving, and you'll probably want to get the hell out of this house and back to your own apartment, but how would you feel about spending the holiday here anyway? I'm going to talk to Mom's doctor about her and my Aunt Marie coming for dinner."

"For real? That sounds nice. But my family..." Kit trailed off.

"Let's invite them, too." Alden stroked a hand over the firm ridges of Kit's abs. "I'm actually a really good cook."

"I know you are." Kit sighed, his chest lifting Alden's head with it. "I'll talk to them about it."

"Please do."

"They'll stay in a hotel if they visit. The girls are really loud."

"Okay."

"You really want my whole family up in your space?"

"I want you up in my space. And they'll dilute the Aunt Marie problem."

"Dilute the—?

"Let's talk about that later."

Alden rolled, careful not to jostle Kit's knee, until he was on top of Kit, pressing his hard dick into Kit's. He lowered his lips to Kit's and heard the book hit the floor just moments before Kit's arms came around him and his tongue swept across Alden's lower lip.

This part always came easy. Hips grinding together, heat rising quickly between them as they sought friction and texture.

Talking about it wasn't easy, but like this? Like this, he could show Kit how he felt.

Kit gasped for air and then murmured "I want to taste you."

Alden groaned. Kit's mouth was heaven. What had he done to deserve it? He pushed down his pants but left his briefs in place. Kit's eyes lit up as Alden moved up his body to kneel over his face. Hot breath through cotton. Kit's hand between his legs, teasing at his balls. Alden braced his hands on the headboard, closed his eyes, and tried to turn off his brain. Kit shoved the cotton briefs away and took Alden deep, his moan rumbling around and through Alden. Hands nudged his ass, and Alden began to thrust, slowly, savoring the wet noises and the rough vibration of Kit's voice around him.

He opened his eyes and looked down into Kit's face—open, trusting, eyes glazed with lust and soft with affection. The effect was almost instantaneous—a sharp climb, and he was right there. Too soon—because he wanted to live in this moment right here. "I'm gonna come," he whispered.

Kit's hands nudged his ass again, pushing him deeper. Pleasure swept across his senses, hot on his skin and in his veins, prickling the hairs on his neck to stand on end as he surged forward and spent himself in Kit's miraculous mouth.

He tried to catch his breath as he slipped free, his eyes closed and his chest heaving. Beneath him, Kit shuddered and cried out. The knowledge that Kit had been jerking himself off while blowing Alden sent an aftershock through his body and another wet spurt from the tip of his dick. He opened his eyes just in time to see Kit's tongue steal out to lick it away.

Alden groaned at that soft touch. This was too much, too good, too perfect.

"That was so good." He eased himself back down to the bed and stroked a hand through Kit's curly hair. "You're incredible."

"That was the hottest blow job I've ever given." Kit's voice was hoarse, and Alden immediately reached to touch his lips.

"Did I hurt you?"

Kit shook his head and kissed Alden's fingertips. "I liked it." He gestured at the come cooling on his stomach. "A lot."

"I wish you'd saved that for me," Alden murmured, easing his arms around Kit's waist. "I want to make you feel good."

"You do. Every time." Kit's hand traced the anchor on Alden's forearm. Instead of tickling, it felt warm and soothing. "You're so good to me."

The praise sent another shudder through Alden. "Can I sleep in here with you?"

"Of course." Kit rolled onto his side and faced Alden. "I wish you would every night," he whispered.

"I can't," Alden whispered back, even though it was all he wanted, too. But Kit had drawn the boundaries of this relationship, and Alden wasn't going to cross them. "I need my space."

Something in Kit's eyes shuttered and sadness seeped into his face. "I wish I could make everything safe for you."

"You do." Alden smiled. "As much as anyone or anything else in my life, you make me feel safe." He kissed Kit's forehead. "I'll be right back."

He returned to his room and changed into a pair of pajama pants, then took his meds. He made his rounds of the house, testing the doors and turning off the lights. He poured two glasses of water and carried them to Kit's bedroom and left them on the bedside tables. Then he went to the en suite and ran a washcloth under warm water to bring back to Kit.

"You made a mess," he teased, and Kit smiled.

"So, clean me up."

Kit folded his arms behind his head and watched as Alden cleaned the come from his belly and wiped his dick. It hardened partially in his hand and Alden raised an eyebrow at Kit.

"Completely automatic response," Kit murmured.

Smiling, Alden tossed the washcloth into the laundry and climbed back into bed, fighting the urge to tell Kit everything he really felt, to just put it all there between them and let Kit do what he would with it. Instead, he turned out the lights and held the man who had come to mean everything to him, and he let the soft beat of Kit's heart and the rise and fall of his chest lull him to sleep.

FOURTEEN

Kit's stomach churned with nerves and his hands shook as he waited for the anesthesiologist to come in. Alden placed one hand over his, stilling them. The IV port itched, and Alden seemed to know exactly how to hold his hand without jostling it.

"You're going to be just fine." Those pale eyes stared into his, and Kit swallowed hard and nodded.

"I can't believe you're here," he rasped. "Tending to *my* nerves."

Alden smiled tightly. "Trust me, the good doctor is going to give you something even better than the shit I take. And when you wake up, you'll have a working ACL again. You'll be walking before you know it."

And then he'd have no reason to stay.

The words remained unspoken between them, but Kit knew: as soon as he was walking unassisted and driving, he would be going home, and this interlude of affection and sex would be over. Oh, they'd stay friends, because that's who Kit was: always affable, always friendly, always the good buddy. When nothing ever got serious enough for hearts to be on the line, it was easy to stay friends.

My heart is on the line. Kit looked down at his hands in his lap, with one of Alden's on top of them. He could tell him. He could tell Alden he messed up when he said it could be no-strings. He could tell him right now, and then Alden would know. That had to be better than dancing around it constantly.

And if Alden didn't feel the same? The nagging voice in Kit's head, the one that told him he would never be anybody's first choice, that he was gone too often, that a bed was just a place to sleep sometimes? That voice needled at him. This wasn't the time or the place to confess his feelings. Hell, if Alden didn't feel the same, he could very well wake up alone after the surgery.

If not now, when?

"Alden—" He started to speak but was cut off when a smiling woman in scrubs and a white lab coat pushed the door open.

"Mr. Taylor, how are you feeling today?"

The anesthesiologist.

"Nervous." He managed a weak smile. "And glad my stomach is empty."

"Oooh, me too." She smiled back at him. Then she looked down at his hands in Alden's. "Would you like your partner to stay until we take you to the OR?"

"He's not my—"

"We're just friends." Alden spoke at the same time, squeezing Kit's hand. "Roommates. You know how it is."

Kit almost laughed, because he was pretty sure most people didn't sit around holding hands with their roommates, but the doctor just smiled and said, "It's good of you to be here for your friend. Kit, would you like him to stay?"

Kit looked at Alden and nodded. "Please."

Alden's face flushed, and he squeezed again. Kit answered the anesthesiologist's questions about his medical history.

"This first drug I'm going to give you is going to relax you, make you feel pretty chill. You might get a little sleepy and feel warm. That's all normal. After that, I'll administer the general anesthesia and you will fall asleep. When you wake up, you might feel disoriented or groggy. That's normal too."

Kit nodded. "I'm ready."

"Good. I'll give you two a minute." She stepped back into the hallway.

Alden stood up and kissed Kit's forehead. "I'll be here when you wake up. As soon as they let me in, I'll be right by your side. I promise."

"Alden, I—" *Not now, not now.* "Thank you. It means a lot."

Alden kissed him again, this time on the lips. "You're welcome."

Kit wanted to wrap his arms around Alden and hold him close, kiss him deeply, not like a friend or a fucking roommate, but he could tell Alden's thoughts were already one foot out the door. He let go. "See you on the other side."

The anesthesiologist came back in the room as Alden left. "Okay, let's get started."

The surgery was expected to take between two and three hours. Alden spent the first one in his car. There was no way he could pace the waiting room, and the hospital cafeteria was out of the question. *I wish I was normal.*

It had been pure hell watching Kit fight back nerves in pre-op. His mountain man had looked vulnerable in a way he hadn't ever seen before, and it wrecked Alden. He was used to Kit being the strong one. Not the one fighting back panic.

You can do this for Kit. Giving himself pep talks was one of those things Alden's therapist had worked with him on relentlessly. Talking himself through panic to a place of possibility. How many times had he almost backed out and told Kit to call his mother? But he hadn't. He'd found the place of possibility, and it had gotten him here. And it would get him through.

He took several deep, calming breaths. He thought about how soft Kit's lips were, and how gentle his hands were. How their friendship had snuck up on him and now he wasn't sure how he was supposed to go back to living without Kit's gigantic presence in his house and his life.

They would still be friends, of course. Kit had made it clear from the beginning that friendship would always be on the table. That seemed to be enough for him, which Alden tried to understand, but his own feelings were too much of a mess. If they were just friends, he didn't think it could be like it was with Tommy. He didn't think he could stand it if friendship with Kit meant the occasional drop-in for sex and conversation.

He'd gone too long with that being the only way to touch and be touched. And with Tommy, that's all it would ever be. But over the last month with Kit in his house, in his bed, he'd glimpsed another possibility. Companionship.

Real companionship, built on friendship, but so much deeper than that. And it was about to be over.

"Goddamn it," he swore into the silence of his car and looked at the time on his phone. Kit's surgery would be nearly half over now. He took a deep breath, then another. He could do this for Kit. He could go inside the hospital and wait. He could live in a place of possibility, not panic. Kit needed him, and he could be there.

The hospital waiting room wasn't crowded, thankfully. Alden wasn't sure if he could handle that. *Possibility, not panic.* He popped his earbuds into his ears and pulled out his phone. He had a puzzle game he could play that was calming. He pulled it out and began to play, concentrating on the movement of the game pieces and not on the press of anxiety in his chest. It took some time, but eventually, he zoned out the presence of the hospital around him.

"Mr. Kaufman?"

Alden pulled the earbuds out of his ears. A woman with kind eyes stood over him. How long had he been working on that puzzle?

"That's me."

"Mr. Taylor is out of surgery. He's in post-op now, and they'll be taking him to recovery soon. If you'll come with me?"

He shoved his phone in his pocket and practically leaped to his feet. He followed her down a blue hallway, a color he guessed was supposed to be calming. She led him to a room and showed him inside. "His belongings are in that bag there. They'll bring him here in probably ten to fifteen minutes."

"How did the surgery go?" Alden asked.

She smiled tightly. "I can't really discuss it with you. He didn't sign a release."

Oh, of course. Alden knew about HIPAA. "Right, I'm sorry. Real life, not TV."

The smile widened. "You'll see him very soon."

"Thanks."

It was closer to twenty minutes—not like he was counting obsessively or anything—when they wheeled Kit in, wild-haired and chatty. Alden could hear his voice all the way down the hall.

"You're here," Kit crowed when he saw Alden. The nurse pushing his bed put a firm hand on Kit's shoulder to keep him from trying to sit up.

"Kit, we talked about this," the nurse muttered. "Wait until we get you settled."

"Sorry. This is my friend, and I love him." Kit said. "He's so good to me. Isn't he cute, too?"

She smiled at Alden. "Very cute. And I think you're embarrassing him."

"No, he's not embarrassed. He's a sasshooole." Kit drew out the nickname. "The sassiest. He's got a very hard shell, but inside he's very soft like a—"

"Okay, now it's getting embarrassing," Alden interrupted before Kit could compare him to a small woodland creature or a marshmallow or something.

The nurse smiled. "He's probably not going to remember this talkative stage. He's very impulsive, though." She frowned down at Kit. "I'm going to adjust the bed for you. How are you feeling? Any nausea?"

Kit shook his head. "I feel great."

"The morphine is still doing its job, I see." The nurse smiled as she adjusted his bed so he was more upright. "Okay, we're going to be keeping an eye on you for a while. You can watch TV. You can have your phone. You can talk to your friend. Do *not* try to get up, okay? Let me know if you have pain, nausea, anything. Your call button is right here." She pointed to it. "Still with me?"

"Where else would I go, Lisa?"

"My name's Lisette."

"Right. Lisette. I'm sorry."

"Don't worry about it. If I'm not in here, I'll be right out there, or checking on my other patients. Press the button if you need me. Where's your button?"

Kit pointed, and Alden hid a smile. Lisette clearly knew how to handle the mountain man.

As soon as she left the room though, Kit turned the full force of his charm on Alden.

"Sasshole, come sit with me." He reached.

Alden crossed over to the bed and took Kit's hand. "You okay?"

"Wish you'd get in bed with me."

"I can't; I'll jostle your leg."

"Don't care."

Alden bit back a smile. "Sure, you might not care right now, but when the drugs wear off, you'll care a lot."

Kit let go of Alden's hand and touched his face, stroking with gentle fingers. "You're so good to me. Please don't leave me."

Alden swallowed. "I'm not going anywhere, babe."

"Promise?"

"I promise. Do you want your phone?"

Kit shook his head.

"TV?" Alden reached for the remote, but Kit stopped him.

"Just talk to me. I want to listen to your voice. Tell me about when you were younger. What were you like?"

Alden blew out a breath and pulled up a chair. "I was a nerdy kid, but athletic too. I was on the track team in high school. Pretty sure my mom told you about that when she was trying to convince you I was a good catch."

"What events did you run?"

"I ran the 3200 meter, the 1600 meter, and I anchored the 4 by 800 relay."

"Were you fast?"

Pride filled Alden, because back then he really had been. He had dominated the distance events and loved every minute of it.

"Fastest at my school. I ran in the state championships a couple times."

"Did you run at Carolina?"

"No. I mean, I ran, but not for the team."

"Why not? You were fast."

"Because there were other guys a lot faster. Carolina is a division one school. It's really competitive."

"I'm sorry." Kit took his hand and played with his fingers.

Bemused, Alden let him. It felt nice to have Kit's fingertips gliding along, warm and playful and teasing. "Why?"

"Why what?"

"Why are you sorry?"

"Because you wanted to run, and you should have everything you want."

Well, that was sweet. Alden couldn't help smiling, and he brought Kit's hand to his lips and kissed the back of it. "You're very sweet."

Lisette bustled back into the room. "BP check." She held up the cuff and Kit held out his arm.

Alden sat back and watched, the low-level hum of his anxiety ratcheting up slightly. At least he wasn't the one having his blood pressure taken. It always spiked in a doctor's office and he'd have to point out that his heart rate was elevated too because it was a panic response, not high blood pressure.

"Looking good. How are you feeling?"

"Not as floaty." Kit glanced at Alden. "Still a little sappy."

"How's the knee? Any pain?"

Kit looked down at his knee as if it could answer her, then shook his head. "All good."

"Any headache, nausea, dizziness?"

Kit shook his head again.

"Okay, I'll be back in a bit."

As soon as she was gone, Kit picked up Alden's hand again. "Tell me more."

And so he did. He regaled Kit with stories of rushing a frat at UNC and all the other things he did back when he was a flashy, extroverted baby gay. Kit laughed in all the appropriate places, but as the morphine wore off, his laughter became less exuberant. Finally, Lisette gave him the all-clear to get dressed for discharge and asked Alden to wait in the hallway.

"Alden will help me," he said firmly. "I want him to."

She looked back and forth between the two of them and shrugged. "Okay, then." She turned to Alden and gave him instructions for how to get Kit's pants over his bandaged knee without hurting him, then left them to it.

As the door shut behind her, Alden gave Kit a curious glance. Kit pulled him close.

"I just wanted a minute with you alone with the door closed." Kit's smile was tired, but it lit up his whole face.

"I don't think this is an appropriate location for whatever you're thinking about." Alden's voice sounded breathy to his own ears.

"Pervert." Kit laughed, wrapping his arms around Alden's waist. "Not like that. I wanted to say thank you. I know today was really hard for you, and it means a lot to me that you're here for me."

"Oh." Alden blushed. "You're welcome."

Kit cupped the side of Alden's face and kissed him gently, whisper-soft but slow. It wasn't a sexy kiss, but it was something so much more intimate that Alden's breath caught in his throat. Then Kit pulled away. "I'm gonna need help getting my pants on, but I think I can manage the shirt."

Alden nodded. "I'll get your clothes."

Once Kit was dressed, he smiled at Alden and took his hand again. "Take me home, Sasshole."

FIFTEEN

Though it had been years since he'd celebrated with anyone other than his mom and his aunt, Alden loved the frenetic energy of Thanksgiving morning. Getting up at the crack of dawn and wrestling the turkey into the roasting pan. Starting stock for the dressing simmering on the stove. Mixing orange zest and sugar into cranberries, pouring in brandy, and then setting them on the back burner to fill the house with the tart-sweet scent of the holiday. He had his brown noise app playing through the Bluetooth speaker over the stove and was fully in the zone.

Kit, still on his crutches, made his way into the kitchen shortly after eight. "Morning."

Alden looked up from his full stovetop and smiled. He turned and leaned his hips back against the counter next to the stove and crossed his arms. "Coffee's fresh."

Kit smiled back at him. "Just got a text from Kelly. She says they just crossed the state line, and she brought green bean casserole."

Alden tried—hopefully successfully—not to wrinkle his

nose at that. He did *not* care for green beans. "She didn't have to do that."

Kit laughed. "Dude. Come on. These are Southern women. They aren't about to show up without a dish."

"What did your mom bring?" Alden braced himself.

"That sweet potato thing with the marshmallows and the brown sugar. It's my favorite."

Which surprised absolutely no one. At this point, Alden had stopped being amazed at the quantity of sugar Kit could consume and chalked it up to vastly superior genetics. "Of course it is. Sugar *and* marshmallows."

"That's what I'm talking about," Kit cheered. "What time do you have to pick up your mom and aunt?"

"Aunt Marie is going to drop mom off any minute now."

"Your aunt's not staying for dinner?"

Alden felt a pang of guilt. "I uninvited her because she doesn't approve."

"Of Thanksgiving? I mean, granted, colonizer holiday, et cetera, but really?"

"Of you and me and whatever it is that we are. Friends. Roommates. Fuck buddies." Alden shrugged nonchalantly. "Gay, frankly. She doesn't approve, and she said something snide to Mom about it. They got into a fight and Mom got really upset. I didn't want her here in the first place, so I uninvited her. We have better things to look at than her scowling at us across the table."

Kit's normally buoyant expression fell into something soft and hurting. "I'm sorry, babe."

Alden shrugged, turning back to his cooktop. "I'm not. For years I pretended it didn't hurt me to have my mom's family, people who are supposed to love me, all say things like I just hadn't met the right girl yet. Years, hell over a decade. And now you're here, and even though you're just staying here because of your knee, I don't want to pretend it doesn't hurt. Because I'm not the only one it hurts. It hurts you, it hurts your family, who have never treated you like that. It just fucking hurts."

"Alden." Kit's voice sounded like he'd been gargling gravel. "Come here."

Alden wiped at his stinging eyes. "I—"

"Nothing on that stovetop is going to burn if you let me hug you."

Alden set down the spoon in his hand and let Kit pull him down into his lap. Kit's arms came around his waist and he wrapped his own around Kit's broad shoulders. Comfort. Alden closed his eyes and let himself be held for a long moment.

"I'm sorry everything with your family is so complicated. I wish I could make it easier."

Alden let out a watery huff. "You actually do make it easier. It's much easier to stand up for you than for myself."

"Then I'm glad."

Alden stood and straightened his clothes before he got too comfortable on Kit's lap. "Are you up for peeling potatoes?" he asked.

Kit nodded. "Sure thing."

Alden set him up with a bowl for the peels, a pot of cold water for the potatoes, and an ergonomic peeler, and they worked to the soft background of brown noise until they heard the front door opening. A moment later, Alden's mom walked into the kitchen.

"Alden, honey."

"Mom." He wiped his hands on his apron and crossed the room to give her a hug. "I'm so glad you came. And you're using your leg!"

She patted his shoulders and pressed her cold hands to his

face. "I'm glad to be here." Then, she turned to face Kit. "Hello, Kit."

"Ma'am." He smiled.

"I don't expect a hug until you can stand without crutches. How's the knee? I was hoping you'd be walking by now."

"It's healing really well. The physical therapist says I can try to walk without the crutches next week. He wants me taking it slow."

"Good for you." She nodded approvingly. "Pretty soon you'll be running with this one—" she gestured at Alden "—every Saturday morning."

Kit laughed. "Alden could run circles around me even before I got hurt, but if he wants a running buddy, he knows where to find me."

His mom sat across from Kit at the table and chattered away with the latest gossip from the Arbors. Kit laughed and asked all the right questions. Alden marveled over how easily Kit seemed to get along with his mother. He treated her with the same easygoing camaraderie he shared with their colleagues at work. Everyone's best friend.

He could fit so easily into Alden's life that it took Alden's breath away when he dared to let himself want it. But Kit had made the terms of their arrangement clear, and Alden didn't know how to ask if they could change the rules.

Alden was still deep in his feelings when the knock sounded at the door. He shook it off and plastered a smile on his face to go greet Kit's family. He started to take off his apron, but Kit stopped him.

"I'll get the door. I haven't seen them in months." Kit grinned and stood, reaching for the crutches.

"I'm not meeting your family barefoot in the kitchen with an apron on." Alden scoffed. "We'll go together." Alden tossed the apron on the counter and followed Kit to the front door.

To Alden's eyes, Kit was a large man, and he was completely unprepared for the sight of Kit's father. He was at least three inches taller than Kit, with a big beard and a bigger smile. He hugged his son tightly and with so much emotion on his face, Alden had to look away.

Kit's mom walked right past them and threw her arms around *Alden*. "Thank you for taking care of my baby."

He flushed. "It was nothing."

She shook her head, finally letting him go. "No, it wasn't. Not to me, and not to him. You have been a godsend."

"Uncle Kit!" A shout came from outside the house and three-year-old Zoey came hurtling inside, only to be swept up by Kit's dad before she reached her uncle.

"Zo-zo, we talked about this. Uncle Kit has a booboo; you can't jump all over him like you normally do."

She pouted, then immediately tried to hang upside down in his arms and get a good look at Alden. Suddenly shy, she stuck two fingers in her mouth and stared at him.

"Hi Zoey, I'm Alden." He held out his hand, and she looked at it like it was crawling with fire ants. He pulled it back. "That's okay, we don't have to shake hands."

She turned her head into her grandfather's chest, and Alden shifted his attention behind them to where Kelly and her husband Matt were greeting Kit. Beside them, Abigail stared at him. She was tall for a six-year-old, with the same brown curls Kit shared with his sister, and wide brown eyes.

"I'm Abigail." She held out her hand with a very serious expression on her face.

Alden shook it firmly. "Alden. It's very nice to meet you."

"Are you my uncle's boyfriend? Are you going to get married?"

"Abigail!" Kelly gasped, then cringed. "I'm so sorry."

Alden laughed. "It's fine."

Kit hurried them through the rest of the introductions, then his mom and sister bustled off to the kitchen with their side dishes. Kit's dad and Matt settled onto the purple sofa, and the girls set off to explore the house.

All the breathless activity spun Alden's head. It had been years since this house had been full of people, and he'd honestly missed how it felt to be surrounded with family.

"You okay?" Kit murmured, placing a hand on his shoulder and leaning close.

Alden nodded. "I'm perfect. This is perfect."

Kit set the table in the formal dining room—a room he'd barely entered the entire time he'd been staying with Alden—and watched as his mom and Kelly swept Alden up in breathless chatter. He was pretty sure every one of his childhood secrets and embarrassing stories was being shared, but watching Alden laugh and joke with Kelly, he didn't care at all. So what if Alden knew about the time he went to picture day with his shirt on inside out? Completely worth it to see Alden grinning like this while he carved the turkey.

"We're going to be eating any minute." Alden stuck his head into the dining room. "Want to round everybody up for me and open a bottle of wine?"

Kit nodded, setting the last of the knives carefully in place. "You got it."

In the living room, Kit found Dad and Matt in a deep discussion with Alden's mom about the Panthers' chances this season, while Zoey and Abigail drew pictures on what looked like an entire ream of printer paper on the floor.

"Dinner's ready," he announced. "Abbykins, can you help your sister wash up? There's a step stool in the bathroom."

Abigail took her duties as big sister very seriously. She helped Zoey to her feet and led her to the bathroom hand in hand.

Brenda stood carefully, and Kit offered his hand to steady her. From what Alden had told him, it was unusual for her to wear her prosthesis all day, preferring her chair at home.

"You're such a sweet boy." She smiled at him. "Your family is wonderful. I'm so glad I came today."

"I'm glad you did too."

When everyone was settled around the table, Kit took his place next to Alden whispering, "The food looks amazing. You're incredible."

Alden blushed and smiled. "Thank you," he whispered back, then raised his voice. "Judge Taylor, would you say grace?"

Kit's dad looked up, eyes wide with surprise. He cleared his throat. "I'd be honored."

They all took hands and bowed their heads.

"Heavenly father, on this day we give thanks for the bounty you have provided. You have blessed us with abundant happiness, with the recovery of health after injury, with new friends, and with what looks to be an incredible spread of delicious food. On this day, we are thankful to celebrate these gifts with the family born to us and the family we've chosen as our own. Amen."

"Amen."

Alden's hand squeezed Kit's before he let go, and something in Kit softened and swelled.

The family we've chosen as our own.

As hints went, it wasn't very subtle. Kit studied Alden next to him throughout the meal, seeing how easily Alden fit in with his family, how right it felt to have them all together like this. For a moment, he was fiercely glad he still had the excuse of not walking yet to justify staying with Alden. Even if all good things came to an end, he still got to have this perfect day to share with the people he loved. And he was deeply thankful.

"Science Sunday!"

Alden opened the door and Abigail ran into the house, leaving him blinking out at Kit's sister. He scratched his chest and stifled a yawn.

"Kit did tell you she was coming over, right?" Kelly asked.

Alden nodded. "Yeah, I just haven't had any coffee yet. Do you want to come in?"

"No, this is Abigail and Kit's bonding time. I'd invite you to come to church with us, but—"

He held up a hand. "It's not my bag. Thanks."

"Does Kit go, ever?" she asked wistfully. "Or has he given up that part of his life?"

Alden studied her carefully, weighing out what to say. "He hasn't gone since he's been staying with me. I don't know if he goes ever. It's not something we've talked about. For a lot of us—and by us I mean queer people, just so we're clear—It's not that we give up that part of our lives, more that part of our lives gives up on us."

Kelly nodded. "I understand. I always wondered if it was science or his sexuality that made Kit leave the church. Our church in Tennessee is very inclusive. The one we go to here seems like it would be too."

Alden wanted to roll his eyes, but he managed—barely—to squash the impulse. "I'm sure it is."

A horn sounded from the street, and she glanced over her shoulder. "Matt and Zoey are in the car. We'll pick her up after church."

Alden watched as she walked away, and she looked back over her shoulder once and gave him a small wave. He waved back, then went to find Kit and Abigail.

They were at the kitchen table, making pancakes on Alden's electric griddle. Alden came and wrapped an arm around Kit's waist.

"Those look delicious," he said.

Kit smiled. "We're making enough for three."

Alden glanced at the giant batter bowl. It was full. "No kidding. It looks like you're making enough for an army."

"A science army!" Abigail shouted.

"A science army," Kit agreed, then looked up at Alden. "What did you and Kelly talk about?"

"Church." Alden crossed to the coffee pot and poured himself a cup. "She was grilling me on your church-going habits."

"Oh, Jesus." Kit flipped a pancake. "You're kidding right?"

Alden shook his head. "Is there a story there?"

"Not one I can tell in front of my niece. But let's just say I parted ways with formal religion in my teens, and I never looked back."

"I get it." Alden took a sip of his coffee. "I pretty much did the same. Broke my mother's heart, but she got over it."

That night, after Kit's family had gone home to Tennessee, Alden went into the guest room and stretched out on the bed with Kit.

"Everything okay?"

Kit pulled him into his arms. "Everything is wonderful. I'm sorry if my sister made things weird with the church talk."

Alden rubbed his cheek on Kit's chest. "It was fine. Now I'm curious about the story you couldn't tell me in front of your niece, though."

Kit laughed, a deep rumble that rolled right through Alden. "My first boyfriend was the pastor's son. We got caught blowing each other in the church basement during a lock in. Our whole family stopped attending *that* church, and I stopped going altogether."

"Oh. My. God." Alden tried to stop the horrified laugh bubbling up, but it came out anyway. "You're kidding."

"It was, as your mother would say, not a good time."

Alden hooted with laughter. "Kit Taylor, corrupting a pastor's son. I am impressed."

Kit laughed again. "You would have been. He was hot. And he inherited his daddy's deep booming voice, which had me confused for a lot of years. Imagine being a gay kid in Tennessee who pops a boner every time they hear the words 'Let us pray'. What about you, who was your first?"

Alden considered the question carefully. Now would be a good time to mention Tommy, even though that wouldn't answer Kit's question and would probably spark a few more. But he couldn't. What could he say? *Before you moved in, I had sex about once a year when my ex took pity on me? Also, that ex is the guy who hosts the TV show you and your niece watch together on Sunday mornings?* How humiliating. No, he'd just answer the question asked.

"Um, my first was just a kid from school. Another guy on the track team. We never got caught doing anything or have any cool stories to tell. It was a typical high school romance. We made out constantly for about three weeks, then it was over."

"Ah, youth." Kit rolled onto his side and Alden rolled to face him. "Thanks for being so great with my family this weekend."

"You're welcome."

Kit leaned in and kissed Alden. It was slow and sure and pushed every one of Alden's buttons, until Kit pulled away, gasping.

"Can I try something?" he asked, breathlessly.

Alden nodded.

"I'm not sure if this will work, because of my knee, but..." Kit rolled, bracing himself over Alden on his forearms, and lowered his hips down to rest in the cradle of Alden's thighs. His cock felt thick and heavy grinding into Alden's own. Alden groaned at the contact and Kit started kissing him again. They ground together harder as Kit grew more assured.

Alden loved the way Kit felt on top of him, strong and powerful but so gentle. As Kit's breathing grew heavy, Alden reached between them and pushed their sweatpants down, wrapping his hand around their cocks. Heat, friction, a delicious rhythm—all had Alden's mind bending as he gasped and rutted against Kit.

Kit came first, with a breathy growl. His come slicked Alden's hand. Combined with the heat, it was enough to tip Alden over, crying out as he spent between them.

Moving carefully, Kit rolled off Alden and sank back on the bed, grinning. "It feels so good to be on top. I can't tell you how much I've wanted to do that."

"I can imagine." Alden smiled back at him. "It felt pretty amazing having you grinding on me like that. You know, if your knee can take it, I'd love for you to fuck me sometime."

Kit laughed and gestured to the spunk cooling on his T-shirt. "Now you tell me."

Alden stood and peeled out of his own sticky clothes. "Take that stuff off or it'll dry and get come flakes all over the place.""Bossy."

Alden smiled. "You like it."

He made his way down the hall to his own bedroom, tossing the clothes into his laundry hamper on the way. He grabbed a clean T-shirt and pair of briefs, then made his way back to Kit's room. He leaned on the doorjamb, watching as Kit pulled on his own clean clothes. How on earth was he going to be able to give this up?

"I need to tell you something," he finally blurted out.

Kit met his gaze with another grin that made Alden's skin feel too tight for his body. "Come back to bed first?"

Alden crossed the room and wrapped his arms around Kit, pulling him into a full body hug. He kissed Kit with all the longing and hunger in his soul, and Kit kissed him back with a matching hunger. Alden was already getting hard again when Kit moaned low and shuddered against him.

"We shouldn't have bothered getting dressed," Kit whispered, his forehead resting on Alden's own.

"Talk first." Alden whispered back, then spoke as steadily as he could. "Earlier, when you were asking about my first, I mentioned my high school boyfriend."

Kit nodded solemnly.

"There was someone else who was important to me once. I'm still friendly with him."

"Okay." Kit's brows drew together questioningly. "That's good, right? I'm friendly with all of my exes."

Alden blushed, feeling silly for bringing it up. "You're right. I don't know why, I thought it would be awkward to tell you about him. I didn't know if you'd be mad or something."

"Mad?" Kit smiled and rubbed his thumb over Alden's lower lip. "I'm not that kind of guy. Friendships are good."

"Good." Alden couldn't help but feel he'd botched that conversation and should try again, but when Kit started kissing him again, he decided it could keep.

Kit loved the mornings when he woke up first and could watch Alden sleep. It took a lot to get Alden to relax, and Kit rarely saw his face unworried. Except in moments like this. Something about their conversation from the night before kept coming back to him. The friendly ex—Alden had seemed nervous, like he thought Kit would be jealous. He couldn't figure out what he'd done that made Alden scared of that.

He must have pushed too hard at some point and crossed some line. Or maybe it was that spending the holiday with their families seemed like a very couple-ish thing to do, and they weren't supposed to be like that.

We could be.

No. Kit had to stop thinking that way. Alden had never given him any indication he wanted more than this. His boundaries should be respected.

"You look like you're furious with the ceiling fan." Alden's groggy morning voice was full of gentle teasing.

"Absolutely want to murder it," Kit answered, grinning. He rolled to his side to face Alden. His knee barely twinged. "Good morning."

Alden's sleepy smile was as beautiful as any sunrise. "Good morning. What did the ceiling fan do to you? Surely nothing worth killing over."

"I can't talk about it. I'm too upset."

"Well, maybe I can do something to take your mind off it." Alden's sleepy smile turned into a wicked grin as he disappeared under the covers. A moment later, Kit's cock was enveloped in the wet heat of Alden's mouth, and he let out a soft moan. He pushed the bedcovers back so he could watch, and he found himself completely entranced at the sight of Alden palming his own dick while he took Kit apart with lips and tongue. He wanted to freeze the moment, frame it like a photograph. Then Alden did something with this throat while sliding a finger over Kit's hole, and Kit was coming with a hard shudder.

Alden sat up, jerking himself in earnest. He came a moment later, shouting in that way he did, that way that sent a sweet aftershock of lust down Kit's spine. No, this was the moment he'd frame if he could. This one right here, with Alden staring down at him with a sticky hand and an unburdened smile.

SIXTEEN

Alden didn't hear the knocking over his brown noise app, so he was startled to see a text from Tommy pop up at the bottom of his computer screen.

You there man? I'm on your front steps.

Thank God it was Monday morning and Kit was at physical therapy.

Alden waited for that old sense of longing and anticipation and loss to swell in him, like it did sometimes when he thought of Tommy. But today, even with Tommy this close, just outside the door, the wave of it never came. Was this what it felt like to be over someone? He made his way to the front door, unlocked the deadbolt, and swung it open.

Tommy was beautiful—had always been beautiful. His upper lip formed two perfect peaks that had riveted Alden when they were younger, and even now, years later, drew Alden's eye to that friendly, crooked smile. He'd kissed those lips so many times over so many years—but he didn't want to kiss them now.

He met Tommy's gaze with a weak smile. "Hi."

"Hey, Al. You look good." Tommy ran a hand through his hair, buzzed short now, and flecked with silvery gray, and then he just reached out and pulled Alden into a hug. Alden clung for a moment, taking in the feel of Tommy's hard, slender body against his, and then he let go, because holding Tommy was as wrong as it was familiar.

"Come on in." He held the door wide for Tommy to come in and made his way into the kitchen. Tommy would want coffee and an ashtray for the cigarettes he was already pulling from his pocket. "I can make coffee. How long are you in town for?"

"Two days, give or take. Can I crash here?"

Alden set the can of coffee grounds down. He'd known the question was coming, and now that it had, he knew it was a request not for a bed but for a bedmate. A friendly, strings-free fuck with someone who knew what he liked and wouldn't expect him to call afterwards.

Ex-sex.

"I, um..." Alden searched for the words to say "no" politely. "I'm sorry, I don't think it's a good idea."

"Oh shit." Tommy's dark eyes widened as he looked around and took in the sight of Kit's lumberjack jacket hanging by the back door, and the two pairs of running shoes—one cartoonishly gigantic—lined up underneath it. "You're with someone. You're—you're living with someone?"

"No." Alden shook his head and picked up the coffee again, carefully measuring out the scoops, then the water. When he had to face Tommy again, he knew it was all there on his face. All that emotion, and the helplessness, like a sign around his neck. *I've fallen for someone I can't have.* "At least not like that. He's just a friend. And he had knee surgery..."

"Liar. Nothing about the look on your face says, 'just a friend.'" Tommy slid a cigarette from the pack and lit it, taking a long drag. He held out the pack, offering one to Alden, who shook his head again. "What's he like?"

"Big." Alden said. "Brawny, like a lumberjack, but gentle. Thoughtful, stubborn, and ridiculously hot."

"Nice. He's not straight, is he? Cause if you're not hitting that..."

Alden laughed. "No, not straight. And I didn't say I wasn't hitting that. It's complicated. But it's not a *thing*."

Tommy went to the window and opened it wide enough to flick the ashes from his cigarette out into the wind. "I'm jealous. I want a complicated, ridiculously hot but gentle lumberjack available for middle-of-the-night hookups. Whose dick did you suck to arrange that?"

"Mine."

They both looked up to see Kit standing in the doorway, leaning on his crutches, an uncertain smile half-formed on his lips. Heat flooded Alden's face, but he jutted his chin, crossed his arms, and grinned back. Kit's smile grew, then he turned his attention to Tommy.

"Tommy Nguyen, right? From *Science Sunday*? Alden's never mentioned that he knew you. I'm Kit Taylor." He balanced himself awkwardly on crutches, then held out a hand, which Tommy shook, smiling.

"Nice to meet you, Kit Taylor. Are you a science fan?"

Alden rolled his eyes. "He's a field biologist. We work together." Pulling out a chair and taking Kit's crutches, he asked, "How was PT today?"

Kit settled into the chair, glanced up at Alden, and gestured toward the coffee pot. "It was good. Did you make enough of that for me to have a cup?"

"I'll get it." Tommy moved with easy familiarity around Alden's kitchen, and of course, Kit would notice. As Alden sat, Kit pinned him with a curious, heavy stare, the kind of stare that made Alden feel like a biological specimen, splayed open and exposed, but instead of his guts, it was his secrets, his memories, and his failures on the examining table.

Tommy placed the cups on the table, peeked in the fridge and grabbed the half and half, then the sugar from the counter, and set them in front of Kit. "I guess these are yours. Alden always takes his black."

"Kit's got a sweet tooth," Alden said. God, that was stupid. Why would he say something like that? Alden frowned, looking down at his own cup of black coffee. He sounded like a lovesick teenager. He felt like a lovesick teenager. He wanted to kick his own ass. *I'm going to die alone because I'm too awkward to talk about my feelings.*

Kit took the sugar and nudged Alden under the table as he poured some into his cup. Their eyes met, and Kit smiled, but it wasn't a sweet, put Alden at ease smile. It was suit of armor. The knot of anxiety in Alden's gut got tighter.

"So, Tommy, Alden didn't mention you'd be visiting."

Tommy leaned back in his chair and took a long drag on his cigarette. "I didn't know I was coming until the last minute. I probably wouldn't have, if I'd known—" He gestured between them. "Well. That."

Alden squirmed. Tommy was just being honest. Why did it make him uncomfortable? It's not like Kit was some puritan who didn't approve of sex.

Kit turned to Alden. "Am I cock-blocking you? Want me to go take a drive around the neighborhood? Maybe go back to my place for a couple of days?"

To a stranger, his voice would sound casual, amiable even. But all Alden could hear was ice.

"I'm gonna finish my smoke outside." Tommy picked up the ashtray and let himself out the back door.

Alden picked up his coffee cup. "So, we broke up in grad

school. Over the years, I would still sleep with him sometimes. It's just ex sex. It isn't a thing."

"It looks like a thing." Kit shrugged. "And it makes me feel like shit. What do you want me to say? Sure, I'll go back to the guest room while you fuck your famous ex right there in the same bed where we—"

"No!"

"What did we do in that bed of yours, Alden? Were we just fucking? Just sex? *Not a thing*?"

Alden stared as Kit's face got all tight and flushed. Did Kit want more than sex from him?

"I'm sorry you overheard that. I was trying to deflect because Tommy is—an astute observer, and I didn't know how to describe what's been going on with us. I didn't mean it like that."

"So, with him, 'not a thing' is just ex sex, but with me, 'not a thing' is something else? Something complicated? But then, how could I forget. We agreed, no attachments."

"So why are you acting attached?" Alden snapped, standing to dump his coffee in the sink. He didn't want it anyway. And fuck Kit for making this difficult. Alden was playing by *his* stupid rules.

"Fuck if I even goddamn know. Would you hand me my crutches?"

"Why? Where are you going?" Alden handed them over and watched as Kit maneuvered himself to a standing position and started toward the door. He turned back and glanced over his shoulder.

"Giving you some privacy. With your famous ex. Call me when he's gone."

Alden watched the door slam shut behind Kit, then turned and leaned his palms on the edge of the sink. He couldn't do this much longer. He watched the drops of coffee in the sink run slowly toward the drain until Tommy let himself back in.

"I should go."

Alden shook his head. "I wish you'd called. I could have told you I was—shit I don't even know."

"The door ain't that thick, Al. I heard. Asshole."

Alden flinched. "I think I'm in love with him."

"Yeah? I got some advice for you then."

Turning around, Alden met Tommy's hard glare. "What?"

"Do. Better."

"What the fuck's that supposed to mean? Better what? You never complained about how I did you." Even as he said it, deflecting *again,* guilt washed over him.

Tommy crossed the room and put his hands on either side of Alden on the counter, taking over his personal space. "I loved you. I couldn't handle what happened to you. That's on me. But that man?" Tommy pointed toward the back door. "That man can give you what I couldn't. But you gotta ask him for it. You *have* to tell him you need it. You don't get to be untouchable Al in his ivory tower and get the handsome prince too."

"Why are you encouraging this?" Alden mumbled.

"I want you to be happy, Al. I want that way more than I want my dick sucked."

Tears pricked Alden's eyes and a lump formed in his throat. Tommy had known Alden *before.* He'd seen the way Alden became a different person, and he *still* believed Alden could be in a relationship again. Alden wrapped his arms around Tommy's waist and dragged him into a hug. After a moment's hesitation, Tommy returned it.

"He does make me happy," Alden mumbled into Tommy's shirt. "I don't know if I can make him happy back."

Tommy sniffed and hugged Alden tighter. "You can. Oh God, honey. You totally can. You act like you're so broken—but I walked in this house today and your whole vibe is like bef—"

"Don't say it. I'm still a freak."

"I see you like this and regret like crazy I'm not the guy who made you happy."

"Tommy, I—"

Tommy shook his head. "It's okay. Maybe I'm not going to make anyone happy, and that's okay too. I just miss—I miss who we were. Al and Tommy. Two nerdy queers who were going to have it all. But seeing you like this is *good*."

"Nobody ever gets to have it all." Alden stepped away from Tommy. "But you deserve to be happy. Why aren't you seeing anyone?"

Tommy barked out a short, mirthless laugh. "You sound like my mother. Guys who look like me, guys with names white people can't be bothered to learn to pronounce? We barely get to be on TV. And we sure as hell don't get to host kids shows on TV if we date men."

"So, it's the job." Alden studied his friend as though he hadn't seen him in years—and had he ever really looked at Tommy during the years since the shooting had torn their relationship apart? Or had he just taken for granted that Tommy was still beautiful and charming because he played beautiful and charming for the camera? Now Alden looked at Tommy and saw there was a strain around his face to match that in his voice, and his heart hurt for his friend. Yes, he was still beautiful and charming, but there was an old pain under that beauty.

"It's the job." Tommy shrugged. "I'm gonna go. Call your mountain man and tell him to come home."

"Where will you stay?"

"I'll get a hotel room in Asheville. Anyway. I'm going to Maine next week. We're doing a story on lobster, of all things. I thought you might want to watch when it airs. Ocean stuff and all."

Alden smiled. "I'm here for this. Text me when you have an air date."

"I will. And I'll keep texting you about the other thing, too."

Alden looked down at his phone on the counter. His number was as private as it was possible to get. But reporters had ways to buy even private numbers. Tommy would text him to turn off his phone whenever the press found out about a mass shooting, so he'd never have to be asked to comment. Alden never took that heads up for granted. His throat went tight.

"This feels a lot more like 'goodbye' than like 'see you later.'" He nearly choked on the words.

"Next time I'm in town, we'll do lunch. With your guy. Don't blow it with him, okay?"

"I'll try not to."

"Later, Al."

"Bye, Tommy."

———

Kit regretted leaving before he even reached the stop sign at the end of the street. He was pretty sure his little temper tantrum couldn't be explained away by being cranky from pain. And that meant that Alden's analytical mind would slice out all the extraneous bullshit and posturing and come to the correct conclusion.

Kit Taylor, everybody's best friend, was head over heels in love with Alden Kaufman. He'd broken their agreement, and he'd let himself get in too deep, and there was no way out without hurting everyone.

I don't want a way out.

The thought rumbled through his head and he slammed a hand down on the steering wheel. He never should have agreed to stay with Alden. If only he could have just left their closeness on the mountain, walked away before he saw past the surface and let himself start wanting.

If he hadn't seen Alden shaking in the throes of a flashback and been the one to comfort him.

If he hadn't let Alden take him to bed, wringing pleasure from his body again and again.

If he hadn't spent Thanksgiving with their families together, noticing how well they fit, just like he did with Alden, working, talking, and tangling their lives together.

If he hadn't felt the sick, cold slice of jealousy when he saw Tommy Nguyen sitting in his chair, and realized *Tommy* was the man who was important to Alden.

He could tell himself if he hadn't let himself feel those things, he wouldn't be driving away from the man he had fallen for. That they'd be friends. Like it was supposed to be.

But deep inside he knew that he'd wanted Alden since the first time they'd met. He'd been lying to himself long enough. He'd wanted Alden, and he'd gotten exactly what he wanted, only to find out he was in over his head. Because he couldn't be a casual fuck buddy with Alden. He didn't want what Alden had with Tommy. And he didn't want what he himself had with his exes.

He wanted it all. Companionship *and* commitment. He wanted to be able to tell everyone that Alden was his guy. That Alden was his. His fantasy—and his reality.

When he got to his own apartment, it felt completely foreign to him. He tried to see it through Alden's eyes, and he didn't like what he saw. Bare apartment-beige walls, not a hint anywhere that the person who lived there loved anything or anyone. An empty kitchen. A set of dumbbells and a yoga mat collecting dust in a corner. No plants or pets. Nothing living and nothing worth living for.

His phone buzzed in his pocket. He set his crutches aside and sat down on the ugly futon. He missed Alden's ridiculous purple couch already.

The text was simple. Two words: *Call me.*

But he wasn't sure he could handle hearing Alden's voice, thick with concern—because Alden, for all his prickly demeanor and deflection, would be concerned, and he wouldn't try to hide it. Kit had left in a completely uncharacteristic fit of pique, and Alden would worry.

I'm fine. I'm back at my apartment. Have a good time with Tommy.

The three gray dots appeared under his message that showed Alden was typing. Then the reply appeared.

I'm not with Tommy. I told you, it isn't like that. Would you please just talk to me?

Kit stared at his phone, shame and hurt coursing through him. He couldn't talk to Alden now. Not when he was feeling this raw, this embarrassed, this exposed.

Another message buzzed through.

Please?

He took a deep breath, then he carefully typed out. *I need a little space. I'm sorry.*

Space to think. To breathe. To lick his wounds and get over himself. Or Alden. Whichever came first.

Alden stared at his phone. Space.

He scowled. Kit didn't need space. He needed to talk to Alden. At least, Alden needed to talk to him. Tommy was right about one thing. Alden had to ask for what he wanted from Kit.

What he needed.

Kit in his bed wasn't enough, though God knew Alden wanted that. Wanted to wake up wrapped up against that brick wall of a chest. Wanted to watch the way Kit's eyes darkened with lust as slow touches and whispered dirty talk made him desperate and needy. Wanted to bury himself so deep in Kit's body he ended up in his heart.

But he *needed* Kit making popcorn over his stove. Kit sprawling on the sofa with a paperback in his hand, voraciously devouring every gay urban fantasy he could find on Alden's bookshelf. Kit calling into their weekly staff meeting through an app on his laptop and scooting his chair close so he and Alden could share the screen. Kit making tea that smelled like bitter flowers and trying to convince Alden it would help him sleep.

Kit pressing his lips to the scars on Alden's skin, and his comfort to the ones on Alden's soul.

There was a lump in Alden's throat when he called his therapist's office to schedule an appointment early, before their regularly scheduled semi-monthly appointment. He hung up before pressing the number that would connect him to the scheduling desk.

He didn't know how to talk about this with his therapist. And oh, the irony. He had talked with her about everything from survivor's guilt to the fear of going out in public and interacting with strangers after two decades of being a cheerful extrovert. She had been the one to talk him through the fear of waiting at the hospital during Kit's surgery and how he could prepare himself and shore up his defenses against panic. He had talked to her about everything terrible and terrifying.

But he didn't know how to talk about how happy Kit made him or about the mess he'd made in his life by letting Kit past his shields. Not until he and Kit figured out exactly who and what they were to each other. And now Kit needed *space*.

Alden would give him that space. What else could he do? March over to Kit's sterile apartment and bang on the door until Kit let him in? Shout his feelings from the parking lot if Kit wouldn't answer? Text him repeatedly until Kit blocked his number? If this was love—this absolute certainty that he and Kit belonged together—then any declaration Alden could make would have to wait until Kit was ready to hear it.

It took three days. Three days of Alden being unable to focus on his work. Three days of staring at Kit's giant running shoes sitting by the door. Three days of wondering how Kit's PT was going. Three days of picturing Kit in his bleak apartment and hoping Kit missed him as much as he missed Kit. Three days of feeling guilty for wanting Kit so much.

Three days of a growing certainty that he loved Kit, because how else could he be so miserable?

On the fourth day, Kit texted him. A single question: *Can I come home tonight?*

Alden didn't have words for the feelings coursing through him. Relief? Elation? The flood of giddiness through his veins was so quick it left him lightheaded. He needed to get the house ready for Kit. He stood and began to frantically tidy up, only to realize that he was being ridiculous, because Kit had been *living* here and wasn't going to judge Alden for doing the same.

He sat on the sofa, the breath falling out of him on something like a sigh as he read the message again. *Home.* Kit had called this house home.

Kit who thought home might be a tent in the woods, had decided that Alden's ridiculous purple sofa was home after all.

And Kit was coming home.

SEVENTEEN

The house was dark when Kit got home—and when had he started thinking of Alden's house as home? When he'd woken up with Alden in his arms and declared that they should take advantage of their chemistry? When Alden had brought him there to convalesce after surgery? When their families had shared turkey and green bean casserole and words of thanks? Maybe it didn't matter when. Because it was home now. And if Alden would have him, maybe it could really *be* home for good. It had taken him all of about five seconds to realize he didn't want this to end, but it took him three days to figure out how to ask Alden for what he wanted.

He looked at the box on the seat beside him and frowned. He couldn't carry it on crutches—and he didn't trust his new knee well enough to carry it without the crutches. He'd only walked without them in PT so far, and it had been wobbly enough that he didn't trust himself on the uneven sidewalk and front stairs, or the ramp leading to the kitchen door. He reached into his cargo pockets and fished out his phone, sending a quick text.

You home?

Alden's reply came quickly.

Yes, in office—I have to finish this report or Dr. Evans will skin me alive at the next staff meeting. Kitchen door is unlocked. Supper warm on the stove. Knock if you need me.

Kit looked at the box again, then scooped out its contents and tucked them into his cargo pockets. Right. At least Alden left the door unlocked.

Inside, he made his way straight to Alden's office door, and he knocked before he could talk himself out of it. When the door open, Alden stood there, rumpled-looking and wary.

"Yeah?"

"I need you." Kit dropped the crutches, grabbed Alden, and pulled him into a kiss. Alden made a surprised sound, but he kissed back with an urgent hunger that took Kit's breath away. Time seemed to slow as Alden's hands skimmed over his cheekbones and buried themselves in his hair, tugging and caressing. Alden pulled back and gave Kit one of those rare, soft smiles of his.

"Thank God," he whispered. "Cause I need you too, and I wasn't sure I could keep pretending I don't."

And then they were kissing again, and Kit's hands started rubbing all over Alden's tight body. God, he loved the way Alden felt under his hands. So strong and hard and alive. He wanted *this* feeling to last forever—not just the lust, but the wild joy of having Alden in his arms.

A claw pricked his leg through his pants, and he yelped.

"What?" Alden pulled back. "Your knee? Did I hurt you?"

"No." Kit shook his head and reached into his pocket to pull out the boy kitten. The critter was scrawny and orange and, freed from the cargo pocket, *pissed off*. "I got this for you."

Alden's eyes widened as he reached out and took the offended ball of fluff. "Hi, sweet thing," he crooned. The kitten yawned, batted warily at Alden's nose, and then started licking its fur.

"And this one for me." Kit pulled the little calico kitten out of his other pocket. "Brother and sister. They're bonded." Not to be outdone by her brother, she let out a plaintive hiss and then started purring.

"Oh, my goodness." Alden touched the top of her head gently, then rubbed his face on the orange boy's fur. "You brought me kittens. You brought *us* kittens."

"You said you wanted to get a cat. The night of your panic attack." Kit smiled. "I thought maybe they would help me explain how sorry I am for being an asshole."

Alden sat down in his desk chair, and Kit deposited the purring girl-kitten on his lap. "I don't know what to say. This is the sweetest thing anyone has ever done for me. But what will they…"

"Litter box and food are in the car. I'll need help getting them in the house."

"Kit, you don't do this. You don't just—" Alden's face crumpled up. "—You don't just get animals with someone unless they mean something to you. This is a commitment."

"I know." Kit leaned on the doorframe and watched as Alden snuggled the two tiny furballs. His heart felt light, light enough to confess, "When I saw you with Tommy, I got scared. I got scared, because he's Tommy Nguyen, and he's famous, and he's really hot, and you were intimate with him. How is a regular guy like Kit Taylor from Nowhere, Tennessee supposed to compete with that?"

"It's not a competition. And I didn't sleep with Tommy that day. I don't want to be with him like that anymore."

"I know. I know you don't. But you were different with him. Cocky and hard-edged and dismissive. I didn't like the way you told him about our relationship. It hurt to hear it like that, even though I knew it was my stupid suggestion that we keep it casual. I don't have much experience being with someone for real."

"Tommy and I have always been like that—it's part of why our relationship didn't work out. I couldn't *not* be cocky and hard-edged with him, and it was worse *after*. He wanted to talk about feelings, which we'd never had to do before. Meanwhile, I didn't even want to have feelings."

Kit took that information in grudgingly. He had wanted to be jealous of Tommy, but he couldn't.

"But you do have feelings. And you have them about him. Don't try to tell me it isn't true, because you are the absolute worst liar."

Alden blushed. "He's the best friend I have. But our relationship? That was over a long time ago."

"I know. I've thought a lot about that over the past few days. And how unfair it was for me to storm out of there and accuse you of—anything. I thought back to the night of your panic attack, when you were so scared and you let me hold you, and the kind of trust you've given me—and Alden, babe, I don't want to be anywhere else but here. With you. I don't need Costa Rica, or adventures, or violent movies. I need to reach across the bed and feel your heart beating. I need to see the way your face goes all soft right before you remember you're supposed to be a sass-hole and you scowl at me. I need—"

"I love you too." Alden blinked slowly, as if he couldn't believe he'd said it, and then he blushed. "That's where that pretty speech was going, right?"

Kit nodded slowly, then eased himself to the floor and put his chin on Alden's knee. "Yeah."

Alden's hand buried itself in his hair and started stroking, like Kit was one of the kittens purring in Alden's lap.

"I love you too," Alden said again, and Kit shuddered. He'd

pushed so hard against the idea of needing this. But sitting on the floor, with Alden's hand in his hair and his own pulse thundering in his ears, this was all he wanted in the world.

"You're going to need help getting off the floor," Alden said softly, and Kit nodded.

"Probably."

"Do you want to go to bed?"

Kit wondered what was on offer—sex? Cuddling? Baring their souls and telling their deepest, darkest secrets? He was fine with any or all of the above. "Can we just sit like this for a while?"

"Your knee?"

"It's getting better. I walked all the way around the track unassisted in PT today."

"That's amazing." Alden's hands ruffled through his hair again. "Tell me more."

So he did. He told Alden about PT and about how cold and colorless his apartment felt after living with Alden these last weeks. About how lonely he'd felt going to bed and wondering if Alden was with someone else. And knowing that if he was, Kit could have prevented it by coming clean about his feelings earlier. Alden's fingers tightened and then softened in his hair. It felt sublime.

And then, when he'd recounted the entire awful three days spent alone being stubborn and stupid, he looked up at Alden and said "Take me to bed, Sasshole. I need you."

Alden stood and took the kittens with him, disappearing down the hallway. When he came back, he helped Kit stand. "They'll be fine in my room for a while. I'll get the litter box and food from your car after."

Kit let Alden pick up his crutches and steer him into the big bedroom. Alden liked taking care of him, and Kit found he liked being cared for. He let Alden push him down to the bed and strip his clothes off. His heavy flannel gave way to an ancient undershirt, which Alden ran his hands over lovingly, giving Kit a look that made him blush.

"I don't know how on earth you and I are the same species," Alden marveled as he lifted the threadbare undershirt over Kit's head. "I'm absolutely positive you have more muscles than the typical human."

Kit's spine arched as Alden's lips closed over one of his nipples, the tug firm and insistent, sending a wave of hunger through Kit. Fingers closed over his other nipple, and Kit let out a whine. "Alden, *please.*"

Alden pulled away from Kit's chest and he dropped to his knees to pull Kit's pants and underwear down. His lips opened and his tongue stuck between his teeth as he wrestled with Kit's shoes, and Kit gave his own cock a long, shuddery stroke.

Alden helped him step out of his shoes and clothes and then took Kit's cock in his mouth with no preamble or hesitation. Persuasive hands pushed Kit forward from behind, and he thrust carefully into Alden's gorgeous mouth.

It felt *so* good, but Alden wasn't easing him toward release, he was... toying with Kit. He kept the rhythm just unsteady enough to have Kit chasing his mouth with his thrusts. Fingertips danced along his crack, and Kit took the hint and tipped his ass backward. He was rewarded by a gentle pressure against his hole. No penetration, just the softest stroke to set fire to his veins, accompanied by a long, wet slide of Alden's tongue around the head of his dick.

"You're killing me—take me deeper."

"Not yet," Alden practically purred as he stood. "Let's get you into bed."

Alden was still dressed, but Kit was completely naked as he laid back. Vulnerable. And that made him harder. Alden seemed to be able to tell too, from the hungry way he stared at Kit and palmed his own dick through his jeans.

"Can I suck you?" Kit asked, stretching out in the bed, careful to place a cushion under his knee.

"Maybe soon." Alden reached down and pulled off his shirt, baring himself to Kit's gaze.

Kit inhaled sharply at the sight. Always. The sight of Alden's body always affected him. How he was so fit without being gym-jacked. The confidence in the way he carried his shoulders. Those were the shoulders of a former track star. Alden's nipples were hard, and goosebumps raised visibly on his skin. He toed off his house shoes and climbed into the bed over Kit.

"The way you look at me gets me so hard," Alden whispered. "It makes me want to earn it."

His kiss was urgent and filthy, and his jeans-clad bulge pressed into Kit's hip with a grind that made them both moan. Kit's hands found the button of Alden's jeans and started tugging. Alden sat up and yanked them off, then stretched his body over Kit's again. This time, his dick pressed through his briefs against Kit's own, hardness to hardness, and they found a dirty rhythm.

"Unh," Kit groaned into Alden's mouth as they frotted together and heat started to climb. "Don't make me come yet."

Alden drew back and looked down at Kit, lips soft and wet from their kisses, understanding in his quicksilver eyes.

"I'll make it last," he whispered.

His weight disappeared from Kit's chest and Kit drew in a deep breath, trying to pull back the rush in his blood.

Alden knelt between his knees, and Kit shuddered. He was pretty sure Alden plowing into him and talking dirty was not going to help make it last.

But Alden didn't pull on a condom and push in. Instead, he

lifted Kit's good knee and pushed it toward his chest. Kit took the hint and held it while Alden *looked* at him.

He squirmed under Alden's assessing gaze. His hard dick strained upward as he spread his legs wide and lifted his ass so Alden could see it. He felt hot in a deliciously dirty way as Alden licked his lips and stroked his own dick through his briefs. Maybe that's how he was going to make it last—by leaving Kit untouched and hungry while he jerked off.

The thought sent another bolt of lust through Kit. He'd been with toppy partners in the past, but nobody with Alden's seemingly effortless talent for making him writhe with lust.

"You are so hot," Alden murmured. "Look at you. So big and strong, opening yourself up to me."

Yes.

Kit shoved the heel of his hand into his mouth to keep from groaning.

"You look like a man who is craving it. Like you would just take my dick anywhere I decided to put it, and you'd come apart. Like you would die if you couldn't get me in your mouth or your ass."

He wasn't far off—Kit squirmed again, and Alden lowered himself down to the bed and delivered a long, slow swipe of his tongue along Kit's ass and taint.

This time, Kit did groan, a deep shuddery thing that seemed to come from his soul and wrack his body. Alden continued to ply him with his tongue, prodding and stroking as a thumb brushed over his taint and the seam of his balls.

"Mmmm," Alden hummed. "Filthy boy."

Pressure against his taint prodded Kit's prostate from the outside, and Kit nearly jumped.

"I love you like this," Alden continued. "That a guy like me can turn you on this much—it makes me feel strong and sexy. It pushes every button I didn't know I had."

Kit's breath caught in his throat at the vulnerability in Alden's voice. This wasn't dirty talk—it was *confession*.

"Come here," he insisted, and Alden crawled back over him so they were eye to eye again. Kit pulled Alden down to him and kissed him hungrily, thoroughly.

"I love you." He hadn't said it earlier, in Alden's office. Yeah, he'd been leading up to it, but he hadn't quite gotten there.

"I love that I make you feel strong and sexy, because you're both of those things, and you make me feel that way too." He punctuated his words with another kiss. "And I will always crave you."

Alden groaned and ground his hips down into the cradle of Kit's thighs. "Can I fuck you?"

Kit smiled. "Anytime you want me."

"That might make staff meetings awkward." Alden grinned as he reached for the condoms and lube.

Kit mulled that over as he watched Alden slicking himself up. Neither one of them had attended a staff meeting in person since before their botched hiking trip. Which meant Alden had been wanting him since—

"How long?" He asked.

"Hmmm?" Alden's fingers slid over his entrance, pushing lube into him with a delicate touch that was so much more precise and filthy than just fingering him would have been. Kit pushed against Alden's fingers but didn't let go of the thread he'd caught.

"How long were you wanting me in staff meetings? I thought you hated me?"

Alden's face flushed and a soft smile replaced the look of careful concentration. "I hated how sexy you were. How much I wanted to do this." A thumb pressed inside Kit, sending a shiver through him. "Every time you showed up, I couldn't stop wishing I were the kind of guy who could let someone else into his life. That I could have a normal relationship." He pulled his thumb away and lined himself up. "Are you ready?"

Warmth washed over Kit, and it wasn't just the way Alden's dick was pressing against him. He nodded. "And now?"

Alden pushed inside, and the stretch made Kit's eyes water. "Now I love you, so I can hardly resent you for turning me on, can I?"

The rhythm Alden set had Kit wanting to climb the walls. Every time Alden's dick dragged over his gland, he felt his orgasm hovering around and over him, one short climb away from bliss. When Alden's hand closed over his dick and started to pump him, the effect was almost instant. Pleasure swept through Kit, and he gave himself over to it, rutting up into Alden's hand while Alden fucked him, relentlessly hitting his sweet spot until he came, his body singing like a tuning fork.

Alden drove in harder, chasing his own orgasm, and Kit watched as he came apart—lips falling open, eyes squeezing shut, and a quiet "Fuck," gasped out between shaky breaths.

Kit waited until Alden had eased out of him before pulling Alden down into a kiss.

"I love you," he whispered against Alden's lips.

Alden kissed him back, languid and sated, then he stood and dropped a kiss on Kit's forehead. He disappeared into the bathroom and Kit listened to the splash of water, then watched as Alden returned with a warm cloth. Alden wiped him clean with the same tenderness he always did, and Kit basked in it, loving how it felt to be taken care of like this.

Then he disappeared again, and Kit heard doors opening and closing all over the house. When Alden finally returned, he was dressed in sweatpants and a hoodie, a kitten in each hand.

"I'm not finishing that report tonight." He crawled into bed beside Kit and let the kittens loose to explore the bed and pounce on their feet under the covers.

"You're going to let them sleep in the bed?" Kit raised an eyebrow.

Alden shrugged, crossing his arms behind his head and giving Kit a languid smile. "Why not? Their hair will get everywhere anyway. Might as well enjoy the cuddles. I'm going to call him Darwin."

Kit smiled as Darwin swatted at his sister and fell over. "And she's Curie."

"I can't believe you brought home kittens." Alden yawned. "And you love me. Will you stay? I mean move in with me, live here for real?"

Kit wrapped his arms around Alden and pulled him close. "I was hoping you'd ask me to. This is home now."

ACKNOWLEDGMENTS

A Kit-sized thank you to Liz, Liza, and Naomi for your early reads of this project and insight into the story and character development. You're fantastic.

Jules, I am thankful every time I get to work with you. You make me a better writer and I am so grateful for the time and attention you give my books.

Vic, you captured the lads perfectly! Thank you so much.

Carrie Ann, you're amazing and lovely and I cannot thank you enough for everything!

ABOUT THE AUTHOR

Vanessa North is a romance novelist, a short fiction geek, and a knitter of strange and wonderful things. Her works have been shortlisted for both the Lambda Literary Award and the RITA© Award, and have garnered praise from *The New York Times*, *The Washington Post,* and *Publisher's Weekly*. She lives in Northwest Georgia with her family: a Viking, twin boy-children, and a very, very large dog.

Connect with Vanessa:
www.vanessanorth.com
vanessa@vanessanorth.com

ALSO BY VANESSA NORTH

The Lake Lovelace Trilogy:

Double Up

Rough Road

Roller Girl

American Heavy Metal:

Hard Chrome

Flying Gold

Blueberry Boys

Summer Stock

The Dark Collector

Hostile Beauty

High and Tight

The Lonely Drop

The Short Strokes: Collected Stories

Reporting In

Rigged

A Song for Sweater-boy

CPSIA information can be obtained
at www.ICGtesting.com
Printed in the USA
BVHW050536040821
613543BV00012B/914